"Belle Barnes—correction, Slade—you're under arrest."

Harlan removed the cuffs from his belt. "You have the right to remain—"

"You've got to be kidding me!" The cold steel encircled her wrists. "And it's still Barnes. I didn't take your last name."

"—silent. Anything you say can and will be used against you in a court of law. You have the right to an attorney. If you cannot afford an attorney, one will be provided for you. Do you understand these rights I have just read to you?"

"Is it even legal for you to arrest your own wife?" Belle tried to squeeze her hands out of the cuffs.

"I can and I just did." Harlan led her to his police cruiser and opened the door. "Watch your head."

He slammed the door. So much for today's happiness. Surely he'd release her as soon as he got back. Harlan wouldn't take her to jail.

Would he?

Dear Reader,

Welcome to the first book in my Saddle Ridge, Montana series! *The Lawman's Rebel Bride* epitomizes two of my biggest loves: family and animals. I believe in doing everything possible for both.

My grandmother Trudy passed away from Alzheimer's disease back in 1998. It broke our hearts to watch a strong, robust woman who went on daily walks with her beloved schnauzer, Dukie, lose her memories. The day she stopped recognizing me was one I'll never forget. It hurts seeing someone you love so dearly begin to fade. You'll do anything in that moment to hold on to what's left. This book allowed me to bring Grammy home, if only for a little while.

My inspiration for the animals in *The Lawman's Rebel Bride* came from The Gentle Barn in California and Tennessee along with Goats of Anarchy in New Jersey. These are two amazing rescues with multiple locations devoted to teaching kindness and compassion toward animals.

As Harlan and Belle evolved on the page, I envisioned actor Bailey Chase and country singer Miranda Lambert in the lead roles. Miranda's rebel roots and animal-lovin' ways combined with Bailey's rugged good looks and therapy-dog adoration made them my perfect fantasy couple.

Feel free to stop in and visit me at amandarenee.com. I'd love to hear from you. Happy reading!

Amanda Renee

THE LAWMAN'S REBEL BRIDE

AMANDA RENEE

HARLEQUIN® WESTERN ROMANCE

Recycling programs
for this product may
not exist in your area.

ISBN-13: 978-0-373-75767-1

The Lawman's Rebel Bride

Copyright © 2017 by Amanda Renee

Printed in U.S.A.

Amanda Renee was raised in the Northeast and now wriggles her toes in the warm coastal Carolina sands. Her career began when she was discovered through Harlequin's So You Think You Can Write contest. When not creating stories about love and laughter, she enjoys the company of her schnoodle, Duffy, camping, playing guitar and piano, photography, and anything involving horses. You can visit her at amandarenee.com.

Books by Amanda Renee

Harlequin American Romance

Welcome to Ramblewood

Betting on Texas
Home to the Cowboy
Blame It on the Rodeo
A Texan for Hire
Back to Texas
Mistletoe Rodeo
The Trouble with Cowgirls
A Bull Rider's Pride
Twins for Christmas

Visit the Author Profile page
at Harlequin.com for more titles.

For Grandma Trudy.
You are forever in my heart.

Chapter One

"Harlan Slade, you owe me a wedding!"

Belle Barnes stormed past the police department's front counter, pushed through the attached swinging door and marched over to the deputy sheriff's desk. Gasps aside, no one attempted to stop her. She'd seen the inside of the station more times than she could count. And Lord knew her history with Harlan was as well-known as it was long.

"Belle!" Harlan jumped from his chair, almost knocking it over. The incredulous stare of his piercing blue eyes almost made her turn tail and run. He gave the room a quick scan before returning his attention to her. "What are you talking about?"

"I need you to marry me...well, at least pretend to." There was no sense in sugarcoating why she was there.

Harlan cocked his jaw, grabbed the Stetson off the top of the filing cabinet behind him and pulled it down low, covering his thick chestnut-colored hair. "Let's discuss this somewhere more private."

Private was the last thing Belle wanted. Private meant being alone with Harlan and that conjured up all sorts of memories and uncomfortableness she'd prefer to avoid. But she was desperate and she didn't have time to waste on foolish pride.

"Fine." She followed him down the back hallway, away from prying eyes. If only she could pry *her* eyes away from the view of his jean-clad backside. The county sheriff strove for friendly casual and Harlan wore it well. The sound of his boots on the worn linoleum echoed against the walls, masking the thudding of her rapid heartbeat. Harlan swung open the heavy steel door and waited for Belle to exit first. She walked past him into the parking lot. Her bare shoulder brushed against his chest, causing her skin to prickle on contact. She inhaled sharply. Big mistake. The woodsy scent of his cologne transported her back to firelit nights snuggled up beside him. A time best forgotten.

"What's this all about?" Harlan's hat shaded his features from the midmorning sun, making him more difficult to read. His tan button-down uniform shirt stretched taut across his shoulders and biceps as he folded his arms. He stood wide-legged in front of her, bringing his six-foot-one-inch height closer to her five foot four. "I'm fairly confident I'm the last person you want to marry."

That was the truth. She'd already stridden down that white-lined aisle only to watch him bolt for the church doors midceremony. There was nothing like the man of your dreams jilting you on your wedding day in front of the entire town. Belle shivered. It was close to eighty degrees in Saddle Ridge and her nerves were in overdrive. The past and the present were about to collide and she couldn't put on the brakes. Not now. Not when her grandmother needed her most.

Belle leaned against a parked police SUV for support. "My grandmother's Alzheimer's causes her to regress more each day." Saying the words aloud made the situation even more real. "She has no concept of the present, yesterday or even last week."

"Belle. I'm sorry." Harlan's deep, rich voice soothed. "I've wanted to visit Trudy in the nursing home many times but I wasn't sure I would be welcome."

"Oh, you're welcome." Belle silently prayed for strength. "She believes we're still getting married. There's no convincing her otherwise. I even tried telling her we already were, but she'll have none of it. She keeps asking for you and I'm hoping if she sees you, maybe we can tell her together that we're eloping and it will put her mind at ease. I don't know what else to do. In a week or two, she might regress further. I can't promise she won't ask for you again, but she's growing more agitated each time she does and you're not there."

Harlan reached for her. His rough thumbs grazed the top of her hands. "I'm sorry you're going through this."

Belle pulled from his grasp. "Don't do that." She didn't want to be comforted or touched…at least not by him. Her heart couldn't take it. "This isn't for me. It's for my grandmother. I don't want to be anywhere near you, but I will do whatever I must to make her last days comfortable, however many she has. And if that means pretending to marry you, then so be it. But I can't do this without your cooperation."

"I'll do it." Harlan checked his watch. "How about I meet you there at noon? Is Trudy still in the same place down the road?"

Belle nodded. The ease with which he agreed

caught her off guard along with him knowing where her grandmother resided. Then again, their sleepy little town of Saddle Ridge in northwest Montana only had one nursing home, so it wasn't too far of a stretch.

"Okay." Belle tugged her keys from her bag, not wanting to be near him any longer than necessary. "I guess that's it then. I'll see you later. And—um—thank you." She hadn't wanted to make eye contact again but felt the inexplicable need to do so. The second she did, she regretted it and turned to leave.

"Belle, before you go—"

She spun to face him. "Don't you dare say *I'm sorry* one more time. I've heard eight years of sorry every time I see you, which is why I do everything in my power to avoid you." She gripped her keys tighter. She needed Harlan's help and yelling at him in the police station parking lot was a surefire way to get him to back out of their agreement. "Can we please do this without dredging up the past?"

"You're asking me to pretend to still be your fiancé on the eve of what should have been our eighth wedding anniversary. Kind of impossible, don't you think?"

Belle's heart hammered against her rib cage. "You remember?"

"August 1. Of course I remember." Harlan closed the distance between them. "You've never let me explain why I left that day."

"Left? Ha! You tore out of that church like your tuxedo was on fire. There's nothing to say. Nothing to rehash. Please."

"Okay." Harlan held up his hands. "I'll meet you at the nursing home at noon."

Belle headed to her pickup, wishing she'd worn something other than flip-flops. They didn't make for a graceful exit when you're trying to walk away quickly. Walk? Forget that! She'd rather run just like he did. If her grandmother hadn't still lived in Saddle Ridge, she would have fled this godforsaken town long ago and never come back.

She hopped up into her battered old truck and jammed the key in the ignition, praying it would start. Money was tight since she'd had to sell her grandmother's house to pay for the nursing home. She had everything budgeted and there wasn't one extra cent to dump into the thirty-two-year-old Chevy. Ol' Red was loud, but she turned over. Belle stepped on the clutch and shifted into first, easing the truck onto Main Street. She arrived at the nursing home a few minutes later. Her boss, Dr. Lydia Presley, had been gracious enough to give her the day off. Working as a large-animal veterinarian assistant meant she wasn't always needed during the day. Nights were a different story. When Lydia was on call, Belle was, too.

"Miss Belle, we didn't expect to see you back so soon." Nurse Myra greeted her as she entered her grandmother's room. "Trudy fell asleep soon after you left."

"I wanted to check in on her once more." Belle lowered herself into the chair across from her grandmother. The woman who'd always been so active and full of life lay frail and motionless. The hospital bed and large safety rails dwarfed her body. Her once round cheeks and flawless complexion were sallow and gaunt. "After this morning, I'm not sure if my being here helps or upsets her."

Trudy stirred and Myra brushed a stray lock of hair away from her face. This was one time Belle was thankful she lived in a small town. Everyone in the nursing home knew her and her grandmother. She'd heard horror stories about the poor treatment of the elderly in some facilities. While she hoped those incidents were rare, she didn't have any concerns when it came to her grandmother's care. Trudy used to be Myra's Sunday school teacher, as she had been to quite a few other nursing home employees.

Her grandmother was only sixty-five and had battled Alzheimer's for the past five years. Early onset of the disease was uncommon and only accounted for 5 to 10 percent of all cases. Belle was well schooled in life-isn't-fair. That didn't stop her from asking, "Why Trudy?" every single day. Her grandmother was the only family she had. Her mother had given birth to her at age eighteen and took off when Belle was six. Took off as in she left Belle alone in a hotel room in Texas, never to return. At least her so-called mother had possessed the good sense to scrawl Trudy's phone number on her left arm so the police had someone to call. Now she was losing the only person she'd ever loved, except for Harlan, and he'd stopped mattering to her a long time ago.

"Were you able to find Harlan?" Myra asked.

"How did you know?" Maybe the nursing home staff knew her better than she realized.

"I'd like to say it was a lucky guess, but Gail saw your truck at the police station on her way in."

Of course she did. Gail was another nurse at the home. Sweet as the day is long, but the biggest gossip Saddle Ridge ever saw.

"He said he'd stop by later."

Myra nodded, not pressing for further details. Belle was too anxious to sit around waiting for the hour of doom. She kissed her grandmother goodbye and told Myra she'd see her later. She had a few guests staying at her apartment and she needed to make sure they weren't wrecking the place.

AT NOON, Harlan parked his police SUV outside the nursing home. He dug into his pocket for a roll of antacids. Tearing the foil open, he popped a couple in his mouth. The three cups of coffee he'd drunk earlier were burning a hole in his chest. Steeling his nerves, he pried himself from the vehicle and made his way to the front entrance.

He removed his hat as he opened the door and looked around. Maybe it was his imagination, but the nursing home seemed too quiet as he approached the front desk.

"May I help you?" the woman behind it asked.

"Hi," he squeaked. Well, that was embarrassing. He cleared his throat and tried again. "I'm Harlan Slade and I'm here to see Gertrude Barnes. Belle Barnes is expecting me."

"Oh! You're the guy." A lightning bolt of recognition lit her face. She'd heard of him and presumably not in a favorable way. "She's waiting for you in room 219. Down the hall, last room on the right."

Pretending to be Belle's husband—even for a few minutes—was damn close to a root canal without anesthesia. Not because he hated her. He wished it were that simple. No, Harlan had been cursed with still loving her. She'd put every ounce of faith and trust in him since the day they met in first grade. And instead of marrying Belle as planned, he'd knocked up her maid of honor.

He'd run out on their wedding because he was nineteen and nowhere near ready to be tied down. Only he ended up married to Belle's best friend a few months later. Correction, former best friend. And he certainly didn't do it out of love. It had been one hundred percent obligation and it came back to bite him in the ass. Molly walked out of their lives within a year, leaving him to raise their daughter alone. Which suited him fine. He'd rather raise his child in a happy, single-parent home than with a woman who blamed their little girl for ruining her life.

"Mind if I come in?" Harlan poked his head in the room. Belle jumped as if a mousetrap had gone off under her chair.

"Not at all." Trudy beamed from her bed. "I've been waiting for you. Come sit with me." She weakly motioned to a chair on the other side of the bed. Her appearance took him by surprise, but he tried not to show it. She'd always been a robust woman. The last time he'd seen her, she'd taken Dukie—her beloved schnauzer—for one of their mile-long hikes. The woman before him was almost unrecognizable.

"Hey, babe." He set his hat on the table next to Belle, leaned in and gave her a quick kiss on the cheek.

The steel daggers that shot from Belle's icy blue eyes were just about enough to knock him dead on the floor. Okay, so he didn't need to kiss her, but he wanted their relationship to look believable.

"Belle, what's the matter with you? Give your husband-to-be a hug. Only one more day." Trudy clapped. "I can't wait."

Belle plastered a smile across her face and rose from her chair. Even in faded jeans, flip-flops and a plain white tank top, she looked like a million bucks. He used to call her his *platinum angel*. When the sunlight hit her long blond hair just so, she had an ethereal glow about her. He caught a glimpse of it this morning.

She wrapped her arms around his neck and gave it a squeeze. A little too much of one if you asked him. The scent of lavender vanilla filled his nostrils. Some things never changed. She still used the same shampoo.

"Make this quick," she whispered in his ear. Her warm breath against his skin sent a shiver down his spine and straight to his... Nope, he needed to focus on the job he'd come to do. She released her choke hold and entwined her fingers in his. Her death grip almost brought him to his knees. "Grammy, Harlan and I would rather get married at the courthouse instead of having a big wedding."

"Nonsense." Trudy waved her hand. "I've already paid for everything."

The comment was a harsh reminder of the money Trudy had shelled out for the first wedding that had never happened. He had tried to repay her, but she refused to take it. Telling him to keep it for the baby. And that cut him even deeper.

"It's not that, Trudy." Harlan's mind raced for an excuse. "The church is double-booked tomorrow and we can't get married there."

"What do you mean double-booked?" Trudy scowled. "I've been a member of that church since I came to this country as a child. Everyone knows tomorrow is your wedding day."

Belle stood there shaking her head. So, it wasn't the best excuse, but she hadn't offered any other suggestions either.

"You two are getting married tomorrow," Trudy shouted. She shoved the covers aside and shook the bed's safety rails. "Let me out of this contraption. I told you people I'm fine to walk. It's only a bruised hip."

Belle rushed to her grandmother's side before she took a dive over the edge. "Grammy, you have to stay in bed." She looked to Harlan for help. "She thinks she's in the hospital after that bad fall she had a few weeks before our wedding."

"Why are you talking like I'm not here?" Trudy stopped fighting against her and sat up in bed. "I fell and I *am* in the hospital." Trudy looked around the room. "I've had enough of this place. I want to go home."

Harlan moved to stand beside Belle and attempted to cover Trudy's bare legs with a sheet. The older woman had gone from zero to overdrive in a matter of seconds.

Belle reached for the call button and pressed it. "I know you do, Grammy. You will. You'll go home soon."

A nurse came in and helped ease Trudy back against the bed. She adjusted it into a reclining position and double-checked the safety rails. Another woman entered the room and stood in the corner, silently watching.

"Stop fussing over me." She swatted both women away. "Go to the church and straighten out this wedding business. You tell them I booked the date first and you're getting married there tomorrow."

"Okay, Grammy. We will." Belle removed her handbag from the back of the chair and slung it over her shoulders. "I love you. We'll go now." Belle ran from the room.

"I'll see you tomorrow, Trudy." Harlan grabbed his hat and headed down the hall in search of Belle. When he reached the front desk, the woman who'd greeted him earlier pointed to a side door. He found Belle sitting in a white rocker on the covered veranda staring toward the blue-gray mountains of the Swan Range.

Her gaze met his as he approached. "I don't know how to watch her slip away like this." Her fingers trembled in her lap as his own ached to brush away the lone tear trailing down her cheek before she averted her gaze.

He crouched in front of her and held her hands between his own. He expected her to recoil from his touch as she had earlier, but instead she turned her hands upward and gripped his. The longing to tug her into his arms and soothe her pain took him by surprise. He hadn't come within a street's width of Belle in eight years, and in a matter of a few hours her skin had seared him multiple times like a branding iron on a steer's rump.

"I'm here for you." His thumbs slid across the soft warmth of her inner wrists. "Whether you want me to be or not."

Harlan sympathized with her anguish. He'd lost his father four years ago and as terrible as that had been, he couldn't fathom having to watch his last remaining relative slowly slip away. It was only a matter of time before Belle would be alone. In many respects, she already was. He couldn't—wouldn't—allow her to face that grief on her own.

"I appreciate it and thank you for coming here." A dry sob stuck in her throat. "I guess it was a waste."

"Excuse me." The woman who had been in Trudy's room a few minutes earlier approached them. "We haven't met yet. I'm Samantha Frederick, the new director here. I hope I'm not overstepping, but I overheard your dilemma. It's not much, and nowhere near as beautiful as your church would have been, but you're welcome to get married here tomorrow. We don't have the space for a big reception, but the garden is in full bloom and you wouldn't have to do anything to it. Reverend Grady is here now and I just spoke with him. He said he'd be happy to perform the ceremony. It will allow your grandmother to be a part of your wedding."

"Oh!" Belle laughed.

Harlan stood, unable to hold back a chuckle of his own at the irony of the situation. "That's sweet of you."

"But completely unnecessary," Belle interjected.

"Well, wait a minute." Harlan tapped Belle's shoulder. "It's not a bad idea. Let's at least give it some thought."

"Please do." Samantha smiled. "My office is next to the front desk. Come see me when you've decided. We'd love to have you."

"Thank you." Harlan removed his phone from his pocket. Tomorrow was Tuesday and he didn't have any court dates planned. He reasoned Sheriff Parker would give him the day off to get married.

"Harlan, we can't do this."

"Why not?" He knew the idea sounded crazy, but it was only temporary. "We'll stay married until—" He hated saying the words knowing they'd hurt Belle. "Until your grandmother's memories fade. What's a few months or even a year?"

"More like a few weeks at the rate she's regressing." Belle stared at her hands.

"However long, we'll get married, live our separate lives like we already do. We'll meet up here and visit her together, and then we'll have it annulled."

"How will we explain the lack of guests?"

"We can ask the employees to fill in for a few minutes. It will be fast."

Belle stared up at him. "We can't get a marriage license by tomorrow."

"There's no waiting period in Montana, but we would need to see the county clerk before she leaves today. If we sign the blood test waiver, we'll be good to go. Besides, like you said, I owe you a wedding. It's the least I can do."

"Or we can hire a fake reverend," Belle said.

"We could." Harlan crouched down in front of her

again. "But knowing you the way I do—or the way I used to—I think lying to your grandmother about something this big would bother you. I saw the look on your face in there when you told her she'll go home soon. You hated lying to her. I don't think you'd go through with this if it wasn't real."

"I would go through hell to make my grandmother happy."

"There you have it. What's more hellacious than marrying me on our not-so-wedding anniversary?"

"Ha!" Belle held out her hand to him. "You've got that right."

He took her hand between both of his, causing her to shake her head. "What?"

"It's supposed to be a handshake, Harlan." She withdrew her hand and offered it again. "We're making a deal, so let's shake on it. And in case I don't say it later, thank you for doing this."

This was the second craziest thing Harlan had ever done. The first had been walking out on Belle. "Let's get hitched."

Chapter Two

Belle didn't like to wait. She hated it. Utterly despised it. Waiting meant something bad was about to happen. She'd waited for her mom to come back to the hotel room and she never had. She'd waited for Harlan in the church and he had never returned. Here she was, waiting once again on her wedding day. Granted she was there three hours early, but that was only at her grandmother's insistence. Trudy may have forgotten many things, but every last detail of Belle and Harlan's wedding remained fresh in her mind. A little too fresh. What made Belle think she could possibly go through with marrying Harlan? Any recollection of their first wedding left her stomach in knots.

"You look beautiful, Bubbe." Her grandmother had been calling her Bubbe, short for *bubbeleh*, since the day she picked her up in Texas. It meant *darling* and was Trudy's little term of endearment reserved solely for Belle. Something so simple and yet she knew she would miss it one day soon. Trudy would regress to a point where she no longer remembered her. Belle's heart physically ached at the thought. "I loved that dress on you the moment we saw it in the store."

Dress shopping with Trudy had been her favorite part of planning her original wedding. She'd tried on countless gowns while her grandmother waited patiently. The instant she stepped into the simple strapless A-line with delicate bodice beading, she knew it was *the dress*.

As beautiful as the gown was, Belle wanted to tear it off and burn it. She'd attempted to once, but her grandmother told her she would one day regret that decision. So she packed it away and stored it in a cold dark corner of the basement with the wedding rings. When she cleaned out Trudy's house, she'd contemplated throwing the dress out. Thinking someone might have better luck with it, she opted to consign it. Six months later, the shop returned the dress to her when it hadn't sold. It had been sitting in a storage unit with some of her grandmother's belongings ever since. After Trudy had drilled her over its whereabouts first thing this morning, she'd spent an hour climbing around the storage unit until she found the blasted thing. She had hoped it wouldn't still fit. Unlucky for her, it did.

"I can't believe you wanted to wear a sundress today."

"Grammy, it's hot out. It was only a suggestion." Belle flashed back to the morning of her first wedding. She'd been so happy and thrilled to begin a new life with Harlan.

Today brought a fresh start in a different way—a sense of closure. And she needed that to rid herself finally of the man she loved. Well, once loved. Her heart had slammed the door on that emotion long ago.

"You're putting your hair up, right?" her grandmother asked.

"Yes." Belle stared at her reflection in the mirror. She had to pull herself together and tamp down the desire to run for the nearest exit. If only she could draw the curtain on the disastrous movie of her first wedding that kept replaying in her head. Thankfully they weren't doing this in the church again. Belle had her limits and that would have pushed them to the max. She inhaled deep, summoning the strength and courage to get through the day and make her grandmother happy. Grabbing a brush and bobby pins from her bag, she gathered her hair into a low ponytail. "I'm wearing it in a French twist."

"I loved that style the best out of all the ones Matilda showed us. Too bad she came down with a cold this morning."

Matilda had been her grandmother's hairdresser since the beginning of time. She'd been the master of the updo, but had died three years earlier.

"That's all right, I can manage." Despite her nerves about facing Harlan again wearing the same dress, with the same hairstyle, holding the same rings and set to recite the same vows, she enjoyed these quiet moments with her grandmother. She didn't know how many more they had left. As painful as reliving the past was, she wouldn't trade it in for anything in the world. She'd always thought it was impossible to turn back the hands of time, but that wasn't entirely true. Now if she could only figure out how to stop time, she'd be set.

Samantha had become an impromptu wedding planner, buzzing around the nursing home and getting all the ambulatory residents ready to attend the ceremony. She even found time to put together a lovely bridal bouquet of fresh cut flowers from the garden. A few times, Belle had to remind herself that none of it was real.

Samantha popped her head in the door. "Are you ready? Your groom is waiting."

This was the day she wished Harlan hadn't shown up.

"I'm ready," she lied. No amount of primping would make her ready either. At least she looked the part. A nurse's aide came in and helped Trudy into a wheelchair. The walk down the corridor to the garden seemed a mile long. Her stomach twisted as Myra opened the door. And that's when she saw them.

"Who invited all those people?" She glared at Myra.

"We thought you did," Myra whispered as the aide and Trudy passed them. "We'll be right there," she said to Trudy.

"I did no such thing." Belle's pulse quickened. "We wanted to keep this quiet." But they knew. They *all* knew. Probably thanks to the county clerk, Harlan's boss, most of the nurses and the residents at the facility. When you get married in a small town, everybody knows. "Close the door." Belle collapsed against the corridor wall, gasping for air. "I can't do this."

"Yes, you can." Myra removed a handkerchief from her pocket and dabbed Belle's forehead. "Far be it from me to pry, but I think I've known you long enough to understand why you're marrying the man you should have castrated years ago. You and Harlan both got caught up in the charade for Trudy's sake. Despite the insanity of it, I admire the sacrifice you're making for her."

"Now we're deceiving everyone." Belle paced the small area. "This should have been a personal moment meant for my grandmother. One we'd quietly undo later. Do you realize how many people will be furious with us when we have this annulled? There better not be presents out there."

Myra pocketed her handkerchief. "You can return them." She opened the door again and smiled. "Now hide your crazy and get out there before Trudy wonders where you are."

Belle blew out a breath along with a handful of expletives before squaring her shoulders. "Fine."

The second her foot touched the garden's stone pathway, a lone violin played Mendelssohn's "Wedding March." "What the—?" Everyone turned to face her. There weren't any chairs, so she had to walk through a throng of people before she reached Harlan, who appeared more dashing in a tuxedo this time around. Thank God she'd worn her gown. She would have looked out of place standing before him in her discount sundress.

She stood under the rose-covered arbor in front of many of their friends and neighbors. The same ones she stood in front of once before. Harlan reached for both of her hands and squeezed them tight. Fear reflected in his eyes. She'd seen that same fear eight years ago to the day. And this time she had it, too. She couldn't tell if she was close to passing out or throwing up. Either way, she wasn't sure she'd remain on her feet much longer.

"Are you okay?" Harlan asked.

"No, but let's get this over with," she whispered. Reverend Grady frowned at her comment, but she felt too ill to concern herself with his feelings.

"Dearly beloved, we are gathered here today to join this man and this woman in holy matrimony."

Holy matrimony. Holy. Matrimony. The words sounded foreign and terrifying at the same time. She braved a glance at the crowd and immediately wished she hadn't. Her grandmother looked beautiful in her purple dress. It was the same dress she'd worn to her wedding the first time. One of the nurses had taken great care in altering it to accommodate Trudy's dramatic weight loss.

"I do," Harlan said.

What?

"And do you, Belle Elizabeth Barnes, take this man to be your lawful husband…" Anything the reverend said after that sounded like the teacher's voice on the *Peanuts* cartoon. Harlan gave her hand a gentle squeeze at her cue.

"I do."

"May I please have the rings?" Reverend Grady asked.

Harlan's eyes widened as he mouthed *I forgot rings.* Belle shook her head subtly to reassure him she hadn't. Only because her grandmother wouldn't let her forget.

Trudy handed the rings to the reverend and he blessed them.

"Harlan, please slide this ring on Belle's finger and repeat after me. With this ring, I pledge my commitment."

Harlan's intense gaze met hers as the cold, hard band slid onto her finger. "With this ring, I pledge my commitment." And she knew deep in her heart he meant those words. Eight years after the fact, but she truly believed he would commit to this marriage as long as her grandmother recognized it.

"Belle, please place this ring on Harlan's finger and repeat after me. With this ring, I pledge my commitment."

Belle opened her mouth to speak, but her words were silent. She inhaled deeply and tried again. Her fingers trembled as she slid on the gold band. "With this ring, I pledge my commitment."

"By the authority vested in me by the State of Montana, witnessed by your friends and family, I have the pleasure of pronouncing you husband and wife. Harlan, you may kiss your bride."

Kiss? What kiss?

Before she had a chance to even process what was happening, Harlan drew her to him and claimed her mouth. Her breath escaped her lungs as the raw power behind the traditional gesture overtook her. And in an instant, the past eight years never happened. The last time he had kissed her like that was the night before their wedding. The man could kiss. She'd forgotten how much she missed the touch of his lips against hers. She wound her arms around his neck in response, not wanting to let go. Not wanting to *ever* let go. The thunderous applause surrounding them jarred her back to the present. She broke their kiss as abruptly as he began it.

What had they done?

HARLAN HADN'T MEANT to kiss Belle. Well, he had—just not as intensely. He hated the cliché *caught up in the moment* excuse. He'd heard it numerous times on the job and it only made him slap the cuffs on faster. But damned if he didn't understand the expression today.

"Toast, toast, toast," their wedding guests chanted. Where did they come from? And the champagne and wedding cake. He hadn't even planned on wearing a tuxedo until Samantha told him Belle looked beautiful in her wedding gown. He'd made a mad dash for the tuxedo rental place and prayed they'd have one. The fit wasn't perfect, but he was presentable.

"Belle and Harlan." His uncle Jax raised a glass in the air. "It's anyone's guess when you two got back together, but I'm glad you did. Here's to a lifetime of health and happiness."

Harlan clinked his glass against Belle's. He wasn't sure if she was in a state of shock, overheating in her dress or was about to toss her cookies on his shoes. Regardless, the deer-in-the-headlights look didn't suit her.

Belle had looked stunning as she walked down the makeshift aisle. Never in a million years did he imagine she would still have the dress and the rings. She was even more beautiful than she had been during their first wedding. They both had matured since then. If they had waited to get married instead of allowing their teenage hormones to make all their decisions, they probably would have had a chance at something real and lasting.

"What did that man mean when he said he didn't know when you two got back together?" Trudy asked.

Harlan squatted beside her wheelchair. "That's my

uncle Jax. He has a lot going on at his guest ranch, so I guess he got a little confused."

"I never liked that man. Where is Ryder? Isn't he supposed to be your best man? And where are your parents?"

Trudy's questions caught Belle's attention. She set her untouched glass of champagne on the table behind them.

"Grammy, why don't we go inside?" Belle turned Trudy's wheelchair toward the door. "It's too hot out here for you in the sun."

"All right, Bubbe. I'm a little tired."

"I'll take her in," a nurse's aide said. "Enjoy your wedding and congratulations."

"Thank you." Belle faced Harlan. "I'm sorry. She doesn't remember."

Harlan shrugged. "It's okay." He made a mental note to drive out to see Ryder at the state penitentiary in Deer Lodge soon. It had been a few months, but the three-and-a-half-hour drive wasn't exactly next door. He missed his brother every day. They'd been best friends until the night Ryder killed their father. The decimation of his family had been instant. His mother had moved to California shortly afterward and he and his four brothers rarely spoke anymore except for him and Dylan. He missed the family they once were. "I understand. Did you expect this many people?"

"Absolutely not." Belle scanned the crowd. "And I can't wait to hear the gossip once we have this annulled. I'll be pitied. You'll be vilified. They'll wonder what's so wrong with me that you ditched me twice. It will be a regular Saddle Ridge free-for-all. Happy days ahead." She frowned. "They still whisper about our last wedding debacle. This was the last thing I wanted."

Harlan sighed. He'd been responsible for every ounce of gossip. She'd always been an awkward social butterfly because of the past her mother bestowed upon her, but she had been an active part of the community. She had organized parties for friends and had even been on the church's social committee alongside her grandmother. All of that ended eight years ago to the day when he left her at the altar. And then her life burst in flames once more when he married Molly. Belle had become a rebel who'd rather spend her time with animals than people. The rumors rolled off his back, but she shouldn't have to endure them. Not again.

"Then we stay married." Harlan said the words without thinking twice. He owed her. "I'm not saying we have to stay together forever." Although he'd willingly spend the rest of his life seeking redemption. "But a few months longer than we had intended. Then we can say we gave it a shot and it didn't work. I'll take the blame."

"I want to argue with you, but I can't think of a better solution right now." Her shoulders slumped in defeat despite the smile she wore for their guests' sake. "I am grateful to you and for all of this, but I should get home. I've already been gone longer than I had anticipated."

"Is someone waiting for you?" An uneasiness swept over him. Okay, maybe there was a twinge of jealousy in there, too. But why? He had no claim to Belle, except for the fact he was legally her husband.

"Time for cake," Samantha interrupted before Belle answered him. "I realize it's not big and multitiered, but when the kitchen learned you didn't have a cake, they insisted on making one."

If that didn't amp up the guilt factor, Harlan didn't know what else would. He vowed to make an anonymous donation to the nursing home to cover all the expenses for the event. The least he could do was pay for one of his weddings to Belle.

After they cut the cake, Belle fed it to him with a bit too much enthusiasm. Her uninhibited laughter more than made up for his face full of frosting. He had missed that laugh as much as he had missed her.

His phone vibrated in his pocket. He'd set an alarm for two o'clock so he'd be home when Ivy got off the bus. Their neighbor across the street watched her after school, but he didn't want to chance her hearing what happened today from somebody else. He hadn't expected news of their wedding to become public knowledge or else he would have told Ivy last night…if he had found the words. How was he going to explain to a seven-year-old he'd pretend-married the woman he once jilted? He was about to find out.

"I'm sorry, Belle. I have to leave," Harlan whispered in her ear as their guests mingled. "I need to have a little talk with Ivy."

"I'm sure that won't be easy." Belle twisted the ring on her finger. "I shouldn't have gotten you into this mess."

"I talked you into marrying me, remember?" He covered her hands with his own. The warmth of her skin caused his heart to still. In that briefest of moments, everyone around them faded away. Their wedding should have been spectacular. They should be sharing their first dance and celebrating the rest of their lives. Instead the woman he'd never stopped loving had been forced to settle for a charade of a marriage. "It will be okay. We'll get through it…together."

She lifted her gaze to his as happiness dissolved into reality. "Sure, okay." She withdrew from his grasp and gathered up her skirt, rebuilding the wall between them. "I'll walk out with you. I want to bring my grandmother a piece of cake before I leave."

The two of them managed to sneak away and head down the hallway to Trudy's room unnoticed. She was already asleep and Belle told him to go on ahead. She wanted to stay a little while longer. He sat beside her and took her hand in his as they watched Trudy in silence. Pretend marriage or not, Harlan had meant his vows. In sickness and in health was the reason they were together again, for however long. He wouldn't leave Belle. Not with a garden full of wedding guests and not when she needed him most.

IT WAS CLOSE to five o'clock by the time he picked up Ivy. He'd called his neighbor and filled her in on some of the details. Between her chiding tsks, he persuaded her to keep Ivy inside and away from any of her friends until he arrived home. He'd run into some of her playmates' parents at the wedding and by now they were aware Ivy's father had remarried.

"Hey, pumpkin." Harlan scooped his daughter into his arms and swung her around in a big hug. "How was school today?"

"It was good. Why are you all dressed up? Did somebody die?"

Mental note: he needed to take his daughter to more events where people wore something other than jeans and cowboy boots. "Daddy went to a wedding." He set Ivy down and grabbed her backpack. "Let's head home and I'll tell you all about it."

After he changed out of his tuxedo and made dinner, he asked his daughter to join him in the living room. "You might hear things from your friends and I want you to know the truth in case someone tells you a bunch of made-up stories." Ivy's eyes grew wide in fear.

"Relax, honey. It's nothing bad. The wedding I went to today was my own."

"You got married? Without me?" She pouted. "Daddy, why?"

"It's not a happy-ever-after wedding like in your fairy tales." Even though that's what Belle had deserved. "My friend's grandmother is sick and she doesn't remember that Belle and I had dated and broke up years ago. We got married today so her grandmother would feel better. But it isn't a real marriage."

"Is it legal?" Ivy asked. "You always tell me I have to obey the law."

"Oh, it's legal, all right." Now that the wedding was over and he was home with his daughter, the day's events seemed like a distant dream. If it hadn't been for the rented tuxedo hanging by the door, he might've doubted his own sense of reality. He'd been all for it this morning when he woke up, but he hadn't realized how much he wanted to marry Belle. Or how deeply invested he'd become in their marriage. Outside of raising his daughter and becoming a deputy sheriff, nothing else had felt more right to him.

"Is her grandma dying?"

"Yes, she is."

"Then you did the right thing." Ivy climbed onto his lap and threw her arms around him.

"Thank you, sweetheart. In a month or so, Belle and I will get what's called an annulment and the marriage will be like it never happened."

"Is Belle moving in?"

It certainly hadn't been part of their original plan, then again, neither was a very public wedding. Harlan wasn't sure he was open to Belle moving in with them, regardless of how much he owed her for the past.

"We haven't discussed it." Ivy sighed and flopped against the back of the couch. "What's wrong, sweetheart?"

"I thought you getting married would mean I'd get a mommy."

Harlan covered his mouth. As much as he hated what he did to Belle, and as much as he despised Molly for walking out on their daughter without a second thought, he'd never resent or regret their relationship. If the series of events hadn't happened, he wouldn't have his daughter. She was the best thing that ever happened to him. He wished he could give Ivy what she wanted. His relationship with Belle was only temporary and he hadn't dated since Molly left. Not that he didn't want to, he just hadn't found a woman he wanted to spend time with or introduce into his daughter's life.

"Why do you look so sad, Daddy?"

Before he could answer, his phone rang. He looked at the display. It was one of the other deputy sheriffs. "Hey, Bryan, what's up?"

"Harlan, you need to come down to the station right away."

He stood and motioned for Ivy to grab her shoes. "Why, what's going on?"

"Well, we arrested your wife. And she's not alone."

Chapter Three

"Where is she?" Harlan stormed through the front door of the station after dropping Ivy off at his brother's house. "And what did you mean she isn't alone? Who's with her?"

"It's not a who. It's a what," Bryan said.

"Again?" Harlan's shoulders slumped in relief. Marriage of convenience aside, the thought of Belle with another man tore his gut in two. "What are the charges?"

"Trespassing, breaking and entering, and theft." Bryan laughed. "You sure know how to pick 'em. Did my wedding invite get lost in the mail?"

"I'll explain that later." Harlan headed to the back of the station, swiped his access card and walked through two sets of double doors to the prisoner holding area. There she was. Wet, muddy and clutching something tucked inside her shirt.

"Hey, sweetheart. I forgot to tell you…our marriage comes with one stipulation. You can't get arrested while we're together. You've racked up three charges within two hours. That must be a record, even for you. It's time to aim for some new goals."

"Get me out of here, Harlan." Belle hurried to the bars and angled her chest toward him. "This piglet needs milk replacer and fast."

"Oh, it's a pig this time. That explains the mud. Tell me the story first."

"There's no time," Belle pleaded.

"Tough." Harlan gritted his teeth. He gripped the bars and lowered his face to hers. "You need to tell me what happened so I can attempt some damage control."

"Fine." Belle huffed. "I received a call shortly after I got home. There was an eighteen-wheeler delivering pigs to the Johnson farm way out on Back Hollow Road. This person who shall remain anonymous said they saw the pigs herded off the trailer into holding pens and the piglet tossed in after them. They said it was a life-threatening condition. I couldn't ignore the situation. I had to do something."

"So instead of calling me or another deputy sheriff, you put yourself in danger and stole it."

"It's a she and I rescued her. I couldn't wait for you or anyone else," Belle hissed. "It was too big of a risk. Especially out there. This pig isn't even a week old and she's sunburnt from being in the back of that trailer for heaven only knows how long. I don't know the last time she ate or even if she'll live. Harlan, either you get me out of here or you call Dr. Presley to come take her. I don't care what happens to me, but you have to help this poor animal."

Harlan slapped the side of his thigh, hating the position she'd put him in. Belle's fierce stare starkly contrasted the piglet's weak gaze. Rescuing animals had always been her greatest passion and he wouldn't have expected anything less of her. Unfortunately, it was bound to adversely impact his job. It had been one day and he already felt powerless around her. Between his past mistakes, a terrifying prospect of a future together—however temporary—and a muddied present, second thoughts crept into his brain. Lucky for Belle, his heart controlled the moment.

"I'm not sure I can get you out of this mess tonight." He reached through the bars and stroked the top of the piglet's tiny head. "But, I'll do what I can. Stay here."

"As if I have a choice." Belle rolled her eyes.

After promising to pay triple the price of a full-grown pig, Harlan persuaded the farm owner to drop the theft charge. She was still on the hook for the B&E and trespassing, but at least it meant he'd get her out of jail tonight.

"Where am I going to put you?" Harlan looked her up and down. "You're not getting the front of my cruiser all dirty. Oh, I know." He strode over and opened the back door. "Hop in. It's not like it's your first time."

"So you're going to treat me like a criminal?"

"Are you serious? Where are we right now? It's either this or you walk."

"You're such a charmer." She scowled as she climbed inside. "I already miss the man I married."

"Speaking of that." Harlan slid behind the wheel. "I would like to be elected sheriff one day and that means my wife can't run around getting arrested. As long as we're husband and wife, I implore you to stay out of trouble. I mean it, Belle. Not just for my sake. It's for my daughter's, too. Whatever you do now reflects on her. This isn't the little secret wedding you and I thought it would be. Everyone knows and I can't allow anything negative to affect Ivy. Do we have an understanding?"

"Yes. I'll be more careful next time."

"Oh, okay. I can see you paid close attention to that conversation." He steered the SUV onto Belle's street.

"Please don't be mad. I did the right thing."

"I'm not mad. You frustrate the hell out of me. Always have. It's like you're permanently under my skin. I made a commitment to you and I'll honor it. My daughter even asked if you'd be moving in with us." Belle's gaze met his in the mirror. "Not because she's scared of you. She was hoping you'd be her mom. Do you have any idea what that did to me?"

"I'm sorry Molly turned out to be such a jerk. I never expected that of her." Her voice softened. "I never expected a lot of the things she did. And I don't wish abandonment on anyone. Child or adult."

Message received loud and clear. First Belle's mom had abandoned her, and then he had, too. If any man ever treated Ivy that way, Harlen would probably be behind bars and Belle would be the one bailing him out.

Harlan parked beside her truck, shut the engine and opened the back door for her to exit.

"How did my truck get here?" Belle asked as they walked past her red Chevy.

"I had it towed here instead of the impound lot. Consider it and the piglet a wedding present."

"Honey, you shouldn't have." She reached up and gave him a kiss on the cheek. He wasn't sure if she meant to be sarcastic or sincere, but he wasn't about to turn her away.

Belle glanced at her front door. "What's that?"

Harlan recognized the fluorescent orange notice without even having to read it. "You've been served your walking papers."

"They can't evict me. I pay rent." Belle ignored the paper and unlocked the door.

Harlan reached above her head and tore it off. "This is from the board of health."

"Whatever. Stand back when I open the door. Sometimes Olive gets a little aggressive when I come home."

Harlan followed her in. "It says you're harboring livestock?" Before he had a chance to look up, a tiny goat hurled into him, almost taking out his shin in the process.

"I warned you." Belle stepped over a baby gate and flicked on the kitchen light.

Now he understood the livestock. "Belle, please tell me you didn't steal these animals."

"First, I'm not a thief." She set a spoon and a bowl on the counter next to a large container of instant milk replacer before disappearing into the other room and returning with a towel. "I'm a rescuer. When people call me, I go. And second, I'm fostering these guys until I can find a home for them. It was one thing when I lived at my grandmother's house. We had room in that big yard of hers. I don't have that luxury anymore."

He had to give her this much—between the small kiddie pool of hay the goat happily lay in, the tiny black lamb standing on his hind legs in a playpen, a duck waddling around the entryway and now a piglet, the rest of the apartment was relatively clean.

"I need you to take her while I mix the formula."

Harlan joined Belle in the kitchen. She lifted her shirt up so he could take the piglet tucked between her breasts. He froze, not knowing how to handle the animal without touching her.

"Hey, don't judge. It was the safest and warmest place I could hold her."

"It's not that."

"Oh, for heaven's sake, Harlan. They're just boobs. I have a bra on."

He lifted the piglet into his arms and Belle immediately wrapped the towel around the little girl. She mixed the formula before withdrawing an oral syringe from the drawer. She tore open the package and pulled the plunger until it filled halfway with the off-white liquid.

"Here you go, sweetie." The piglet hesitated at first, then readily took the mixture. "Thank you, thank you, thank you," Belle repeated under her breath. "I don't know what I'll do with you." She nuzzled the little critter, then looked around the room. "Or any of you, but I'm glad you're safe."

"Oh, Belle." Harlan looked to the ceiling and prayed for strength. "You know exactly what you're going to do. You and your menagerie are coming back to the ranch with me."

AFTER A SHOWER and a change of clothes, Belle and Harlan packed up what they could from her apartment, crated the animals and drove to his ranch. She always thought you had at least thirty days to vacate once you received an eviction notice. Turned out it was only three days in certain cases—livestock being one of them. She pulled in behind him, still trying to wrap her brain around the day. This morning she was single and independent. Tonight, she was married and relying on her worst enemy to put a roof over her head. Maybe *worst* was a little harsh. He had earned significant brownie points during the past twenty-four hours. That still didn't mean she forgave him for what he'd done. She doubted that would ever be possible.

Harlan leaned in her passenger window. "Are you coming?"

"In a minute." Belle glanced up at the white farmhouse. It should have been her house. They had picked it out together and Harlan's uncle Jax had fronted them the down payment until they could afford to pay it back. She loved the house. Had envisioned exactly how she would decorate it. Only she never had the chance to spend a single night in it. Molly had had that honor.

She needed to get it together. The ranch was a much better place for her wards. The previous owner had rebuilt the stables, along with the apartment above it. At least there had been an apartment eight years ago.

"Come on, let's get them settled, and then we'll get you situated in the house."

"I don't think so, Harlan." Belle looked up at the main house again. "Where's your daughter?"

"She's staying with Dylan and my uncle Jax at the Silver Bells Ranch. I'll pick her up tomorrow."

"Is there still an apartment over the stalls?" Belle

dug the tip of her boot into the hard dirt drive. "I'd rather be near the animals. Lillie needs constant care."

"Lillie?" Harlan furrowed his brows. "Ah, you named the pig already."

"I'll have to take her to work with me." Belle began unloading the truck. If she kept moving and talking, she wouldn't have a chance to change her mind. "She needs to be fed every couple of hours and that will wake up you and Ivy. So if that apartment is available, I think it's best if I stay out here. I'll pay rent until I can find another place. I don't want to upset your routine, or raise Ivy's hopes."

Harlan closed the short distance between them and gripped both of her shoulders. "Breathe, Belle, breathe."

She didn't want to look up at him and see the pity he must feel for her. "I'm breathing." She turned away and grabbed the pet carrier from the front seat and held it up. "Isn't that right, Lillie? We're both breathing."

"The apartment's yours. It's been a few weeks since I last cleaned up there, so there might be a few cobwebs. Ivy likes to use it as a playhouse."

They finished unloading both vehicles and set the animals up in two of the stalls. Olive bounced around like an overexcited child, and Samson, the two-week-old black lamb, settled right in.

"This will work out well. Olive will be able to go outside to graze and I need to introduce Samson to grass soon to activate his rumen. I prefer grazing to only giving them hay."

"Rumen?"

"It's a large fermentation vat where bacteria and

other microorganisms live. Sheep and goats are rumi-
nant animals. Like cows. They have a four-chamber
stomach."

"Okay, what's with the duck?" Harlan sat on a hay
bale and watched the large white bird waddle down the
stable corridor, squawking at the horses as she passed.
"She seems old enough to be on her own. Why do you
have her?"

"Imogene can't fly, so she's a—"

"Sitting duck. I get it now." Harlan smiled. "She
can't defend herself."

"Lydia—Dr. Presley—is working with me to help
create a nonprofit animal rescue center for injured and
abandoned animals." Belle picked up Imogene and sat
next to Harlan on the hay bale. "The main goal is to
foster them until they find their forever homes. Finding
and affording the land is the biggest obstacle. I'm hoping I can convince one of the larger ranches to donate
some acreage, but I need to file for my nonprofit first.
My, um, police record doesn't help matters."

"Then why do you continue to put yourself in that
situation?" Harlan asked.

"When you work for a large-animal vet, you amass
an extensive network of animal hospitals, foster homes
and volunteers willing to help give animals a second
chance. I'm sure you experience the same thing on a
human level. For each success story, there are many
that never make it. When someone calls me, or Lydia,
we go. We'd love to navigate through the proper channels every time. And sometimes we can. Other times
it's an emergency. If Lydia gets arrested, she can lose
her veterinary license. I have nothing for them to take."

Harlan reached out and petted the top of the duck's head. "Everyone has their passion."

"Yours is law enforcement. Mine's animal rescue. Sometimes that means we butt heads." Belle stood and placed Imogene inside the stall with Olive. "These two love to snuggle together at night. Care to show me upstairs?"

Harlan led Belle to the studio apartment. It was larger than the one-bedroom she'd just been evicted from. It was nicer than she remembered. Little frilly touches here and there. She wondered if they had been Molly's doing or possibly his mom's or Ivy's.

She'd never met his daughter before, only seen her from afar around town. It had surprised her when Harlan had told her Ivy wanted her to move in. It was one more reason not to stay in the main house. She didn't want to involve Ivy in their fake marriage drama any more than she already was.

"I think I'm going to turn in. It's been a long, interesting day." Belle smiled up at him, not sure what the proper protocol was for saying good-night. They may be husband and wife, but there was no way they'd ever consummate the marriage.

Harlan jammed his hands in the front pockets of his jeans, eliminating the awkward hug she wanted to avoid. "There's plenty of room in the barn behind the stables. We can pick up the rest of your things tomorrow and store them in there for the time being. If you need anything, just ask."

"Thank you. I think I've gone above and beyond my favor quota for the week."

Harlan laughed. "It's okay. I've always said your

heart is in the right place. How you go about doing certain things is a little more questionable. I know you mean well. Please promise me something."

"Yeah, yeah. Stay out of trouble." Belle smiled. "I promise to try."

Harlan nodded. "That's all I ask. I'll leave you and Lillie to it. Good night, Belle."

"Good night, Harlan."

Belle watched him shut the door behind him as he left the room. He hadn't even tried to hug or kiss her. It was exactly what she wanted. Any chance of a future they had together had shattered into a million shards of glass long ago.

Belle ran to the door, threw it open and bounded down the stairs, hoping to catch him. By the time she made it to the stable entrance, he was already halfway up the porch steps. As he reached the top, he hesitated. Belle held her breath and willed him to turn around, but he continued into the house.

Chapter Four

Harlan stood at the kitchen sink and stared out the window toward the stables. Last night he'd summoned an iron will to keep from carrying Belle back to the main house and celebrating their marriage the way a man and wife should. He'd expected the band around his finger to feel heavy. It had when he'd married Molly. This time was different. Despite the circumstances, this time felt natural. And his relationship with Belle was anything but.

He filled two travel mugs with coffee and headed out the back door. His breath caught in his throat at the sight of her. He didn't know why. He'd poured her coffee knowing she was there. But seeing Belle muck the stalls confirmed yesterday hadn't been a dream. She was back in his life. And the fine line between terrified and excited blurred with each passing second.

"Good morning. How's Lillie?"

"She made it through the night and had two more feedings." Belle continued to shovel without looking up. "She's taking a nap before I bring her to work."

"I brought you coffee." Harlan set the mug on a hay bale, maintaining his distance. The closer he got to her, the faster his heart beat. "You don't have to do this." Outlaw poked his head out of the empty stall Belle had moved him into. "I don't expect you to work for me or tend to my horses."

Belle shrugged in acknowledgment. "It's the least I can do. I would have fed them but I saw two different pellets in your feed bins and I didn't know who got what. If you show me, I'll take care of them for you."

"Trying to keep me out of my own stables?" Harlan's body tensed.

"It's not that." Belle's shoulders slumped before she looked up at him. "Okay, maybe it is." She rested the shovel handle against the crook of her arm and tugged off her gloves. "Everything else aside, I feel guilty about not coming to see you when your dad died. Your family has always been wonderful to me and I should have swallowed my pride and tried."

Harlan picked up her coffee and handed it to her. "You did. I saw you at the cemetery." Her eyes widened at his admission. "At first I wasn't sure it was you off in the distance, but when Dylan noticed you, too, I had my confirmation."

"It wasn't enough." Belle averted her gaze from his once again. "How is your mom?"

"Good. She remarried and seems happy with her new life in California. I've only been out there once." Now it was his turn to feel awkward. Four years had passed since Ryder had been convicted of vehicular manslaughter. Harlan still didn't believe the circumstances surrounding his father's death, but he'd been forced to accept them after his brother pled guilty and had been sentenced to fifteen years in the state penitentiary. "I should fly out there sometime soon. I know Ivy would love to see her grandmother. Maybe over Thanksgiving."

"Please give her my best." Belle flipped open the top of the mug and took a sip. "Thank you. You even remembered how I take my coffee."

"Light and sweet." How could he forget? He used to tease her about it. *Light and sweet, just like you.* "But seriously, Belle, I don't want you to feel you owe me anything for staying here. I know we can't ignore the past, but we can try to keep it there. I appreciate the gesture."

"I will still clean the stalls because, believe it or not, busy work helps me think. The sooner I can get my rescue operation open, the more animals I'll be able to save." She plucked her phone from her back pocket and tapped the screen. "Come look at this." She sidled up to him as he entered the stall, her shoulder grazing his upper arm. "It's a nonprofit with locations in California and Tennessee called The Gentle Barn. It provides a safe haven for animals in need while educating the community about kindness and compassion. They even have a cow with a prosthetic limb. Isn't it remarkable?" Belle beamed as she continued to scroll through the photos. "My goal is to provide my rescues with whatever medical care they may require. If I can adopt them out into loving forever homes, wonderful. If not, that's okay, too. Either way, they'll never suffer again."

The sincerity in Belle's voice was another reminder why he fell in love with her so long ago. She did everything with purpose and her whole heart. The rescue was a great idea. Ivy would love it, especially since she wanted to become a veterinarian.

"Why are you looking at me like that?" Belle stepped away from him.

"I have a proposition for you." Harlan feared he'd regret what he was about to say, but even worse, he feared he'd regret it even more if he didn't. "I have more acreage here than I need. You and I chose this property because of its spectacular views of the Swan Range. I think it's only fair for you to use part of it for your rescue. No strings, no cost. We'll call it your first donation."

She opened her mouth and for a second he thought she'd balk at the idea. "Are you sure you want me this close to you and your daughter?"

"Belle, I have nothing against you. And I admit, I am concerned with you interacting with Ivy. She's an inquisitive child and as soon as I pick her up after work she'll want to meet you. Are you okay with that?"

"I don't harbor any resentment toward her." The corners of her mouth turned downward. "I resented the situation and a part of me still does. But Ivy is an innocent child who became the victim of a bad situation. I can sympathize with that. I know what it's like to have a mother walk out and never return. I'll be her friend, but I don't want her to believe you and I are a real couple because it will break her heart when I leave."

Leave? Of course she would leave eventually. But if she accepted his proposal, she would just be on the other side of the property. Granted he wouldn't see her every day, but he'd know she was there.

"Ivy's aware of your grandmother's illness. She

doesn't know the specifics, but she knows enough. I'll remind her so there's no confusion. Does that mean you'll accept my offer?"

"I'd be a fool not to." She exhaled slowly. "And I might be a fool to say yes."

"I have a little over a hundred acres. You're welcome to half of it."

Belle shook her head. "Fifty acres is much more than I can handle."

"I'll deed you whatever you feel you need now, and if you want to add more later, you can. There's another entrance to the ranch on the back side of the property. Start with that parcel. The land's fairly clear and there's already an outbuilding there. I can't guarantee it's not a complete teardown. I haven't been out there in a while. But if it is, I'll help you with that, too." Harlan fought to stop rambling. "It's up to you. You need to be comfortable with it."

Her expression filled with worry. "Are you comfortable with it? Or is this an attempt to clear your conscience?"

"Belle, I'll never escape the guilt of leaving you at the altar, but that's not why I'm offering. I have one major concern. I can't have my daughter affected by your sometimes reckless choices. If you can promise to call me before doing anything rash, I would be happy to help you start your rescue."

"Then I think we have a deal." She gave him a soft, warm smile.

Belle held out her hand. This time he knew enough to shake it. The feel of her palm against his set his heart aflame. A small ball of forbidden desire burned in the pit of his stomach. He wanted to seal their arrangement with a kiss. To give her what was rightfully hers and what should have been hers all along. The land and his heart. But he couldn't. He'd had his chance. If he hadn't bolted on their wedding day, Belle never would have faced half the challenges she'd endured. And she most likely wouldn't have a police record. He'd set off a chain reaction eight years ago and it had deeply affected Belle and his daughter. He might be able to right some of his wrongs, but he'd have to live with the consequences of never knowing what could have been.

FOR THE SECOND day in a row, Belle couldn't believe how much her life had changed overnight. Harlan's generous land offer touched her more than she'd ever admit. At least she wouldn't admit it to him. Was that petty and childish? Maybe. But she wasn't ready to destroy the protective wall she'd built around her heart. Not only to keep him out, but to keep herself from wanting more.

Harlan was an old habit, one she craved with each passing second. She refused to give in to it. She'd worked hard to form new, less dependent relationships. None had resulted in any long-term romances, but she'd learned to value her friendships and stand on her own. And until she saw the deed transferred into her name, she couldn't afford to get her hopes up.

Who was she kidding? She silently cheered behind the steering wheel of her truck, not wanting to startle Lillie. She was over the moon thrilled. Any attachments she had to that property had faded long ago. Or so she thought. This morning had been difficult. It was the first time she woke up on what should have been hers. Not that she'd gotten much sleep, and she lived in the stables, but it was close enough. And it stung.

She drove onto Dr. Lydia Presley's ranch and parked in front of the stables. It was strictly an ambulatory practice, but Lydia used the ranch as home base. Breaking the news to her friend and employer about her arrest wouldn't be easy. Harlan hadn't been the only one warning her to stay out of trouble.

She reached over to the passenger side and unlatched the seat belt. "It was all worth it, wasn't it, Lillie?" She lifted the carrier and climbed out of the truck. "Let's go make sure you're okay."

"Good morning," Lydia greeted her from the supply room. "Is this our newest patient?" She peered in the carrier. "Wow, she is tiny. Let me take a better look at her." The piglet squealed in Lydia's deep, bronzed hands. "Shh. It's okay, baby girl. I don't like the look of this sunburn. She already has a blister forming."

"I'm estimating she's only a couple days old."

"I agree. What did you name her?" Lydia placed the piglet on the scale.

"Lillie with an *i e*. She reminds me of a pink lily-pad bloom."

"She's close to the size of one of those flowers, too. Lillie only weighs 1.2 pounds. She's severely underweight for a newborn commercial pig. Let's start a round of antibiotics and treat the burn. We'll vaccinate in three weeks and begin her boosters in four. You never told me how you acquired her." Lydia raised one perfectly arched brow. "Or will my knowing make me an accessory after the fact?"

"No, no, she's been bought and paid for." Belle gnawed on her inner cheek.

"That's good to know." Lydia smoothed a light coat of ointment on Lillie's back. "She'll need this reapplied throughout the day. As soon as it looks dry again, apply another layer. Do you even have room for her at your apartment?"

"Not quite. I got evicted last night."

"To be honest, I thought it would have happened long before now." Lydia's dense spiraled curls bounced as she shook her head. "Where are you staying?"

"With Harlan."

"Harlan? The same Harlan who left you crying at the altar?"

"I did not cry." Her mind tumbled to push that day further into the past. She had relived it enough times over the last eight years.

"Oh, honey, I was there and you not only cried, you ugly cried. When did this reunion happen?"

"Well…" Belle wrung her hands. "Technically, two days ago. But then there was our wedding yesterday and we had planned to live separately until he had to bail me out of jail."

"Say what now?" Lydia stilled.

"That's how I got Lillie. I rescued her from the Johnson farm."

"What would a Belle Barnes rescue be without a trip to the hoosegow? But that's not what concerns me. Well, it does but we'll discuss that later. What is this about you marrying Harlan? You mean you told Trudy you were getting married at city hall, right? Please tell me you didn't actually marry him."

Belle slid a stool toward Lydia. "You'll need to sit down for this one."

Twenty minutes later, Lydia was still cradling Lillie and staring at Belle in disbelief. "You could have at least invited me to the ceremony."

"It happened so fast." Belle still hadn't sorted her thoughts about the entire situation. "No one was supposed to be there, but the news of it spread. Unfortunately, it didn't reach you out here."

"That's all right. I would have tried to stop you, anyway."

"I know you would have." Despite the fifteen-year age difference, Lydia was Belle's closest friend. "I had to do this for my grandmother. You should have seen her face light up yesterday. And I'll always have that memory, long after she forgets."

Lydia reached over and squeezed her hand. "I can't imagine how difficult this is for you."

Belle fought back the tears threatening to spring free. "Every time I walk into her room, I wonder if this will be the day she doesn't recognize me. Some days she takes longer to make the connection. And poor Harlan. She asked him where his parents and Ryder were. He handled it without missing a beat, but I'm sure it hurt just the same."

"I won't say he's the man for you, because he's not. But if he's willing to go along with this charade for Trudy's sake, then he's earned a few redemption points in my book."

"Wait until you hear what he gave me this morning."

"Oh, yuck." Lydia stood up. "Keep your sex life to yourself."

Heat rose to Belle's cheeks. "I assure you we didn't and we won't. He offered me part of the ranch for the rescue and I accepted."

"And you'll live where? With him?"

Well, that wasn't the reaction she expected. "I hadn't thought that far ahead. I guess I could live on the ranch—my side of the ranch. Maybe I'll get one of those cute vintage trailers."

All Belle's plans had factored in her still having an apartment. And she couldn't stay above the stables forever. It was too close to Harlan. Too tempting to create new memories to erase the old. But the old ones would never die. Her scars wouldn't let her forget even though her heart ached for a fresh start.

"Belle?" Lydia waved her hands. "Where did you go?"

Belle fought to regain her composure. "Nowhere. And there's plenty of time to work out my living arrangements. The point is, I can finally move forward. Are you still willing to partner with me?" A few other people were interested in the event Lydia changed her mind, but she'd always envisioned the project with her friend by her side. "I need two signatures on the articles of association to show its creation."

"Yes."

"Okay." Lydia's terse response surprised her. "I thought you'd be more enthused than this."

"I'm concerned your arrests will kill your dream before it ever gets off the ground." Lydia gently placed the piglet in Belle's arms. "I suspect you and Harlan had this conversation last night. That man has aspirations, too. I'm no fan of his, but it sounds as if he's trying to do right by you. You need to grant him the same respect, despite what happened."

"We've already discussed it. From now on, I am on my best behavior." Belle swaddled Lillie to keep her core body temperature warm and placed her in the carrier. "Last night was an exception to the rules. The other pigs would have trampled her to death if I hadn't acted when I did. I'm surprised she survived at all."

"Do me one favor. When you begin to remember the good times you once shared with Harlan, remember the aftermath, too."

"I promise." She'd never give Harlan that power over her again.

"Okay, then." Lydia handed her one of the mobile supply bags. "Today's castration day. Let's take the world by the balls."

Chapter Five

Belle's pickup spit and sputtered the entire way to Harlan's ranch, reminding her to change the oil sooner than later. She was glad to be home—well, her temporary home. Lillie had been with her, but between the castrations and visiting her grandmother at the nursing home, she'd had to run back to the ranch throughout the day to check on Samson and Olive.

Samson had been orphaned at birth and required feedings throughout the day. Olive was born last fall and lost her ears to frostbite during the winter. She was a third of the size of a normal goat, but healthy and full of mischief. Belle hoped to find her a forever home with other goats to bond with, but until then she'd play surrogate mom. It wasn't ideal and she had to keep Olive separated from Samson for fear she'd head butt the black fleecy bundle, but at least her wards were safe.

She'd picked up a salad and looked forward to a hot shower followed by a relaxing evening. The instant she parked in front of the stables, all thoughts of relaxation ceased. Harlan stood near the doorway grooming one of his horses while Ivy sat on a hay bale, petting Imogene.

Harlan had warned her Ivy wanted to meet her. And Belle was okay with that. She couldn't help but think the seven-year-old should have been hers…not Molly's. Belle wanted kids. She had once envisioned her and Harlan having a houseful of them. Maybe she would still have the chance one day. Not with Harlan, but with another man if she ever found one worthy of her love. At this point, she didn't believe anyone was worth the risk. Except animals. They provided unconditional love.

"Hi." Only Harlan's deep voice had the power to make her body tingle with one syllable. She needed to correct that and fast. "I hope it was okay for her to visit with the duck. I forgot her name."

"Ivy can visit Imogene whenever she wants. These animals need as much love and affection as they can get." *So do I.* Belle shook the thought from her head. "Are you going to introduce us?"

"Sweetheart, this is my friend Belle." Harlan rested a hand on the small of her back, weakening her knees more than they already were. "Belle, this is my daughter, Ivy."

"It's a pleasure to meet you." Belle knelt before the girl, freeing herself from Harlan's touch. "I see you made friends with Imogene. She loves attention."

"She's so soft. I've never petted a duck. Daddy won't even let me have a dog."

Belle side-glanced at Harlan. "Since when are you against dogs? You had a bunch of them growing up on your parents' ranch."

Ivy's eyes widened. "You did?"

"You're not helping." Harlan's lips thinned into a smile. "Between my work and her school, I don't have time to come back here during the day. We don't exactly live in the center of town."

"Tell me about it." It was one of the reasons she and Harlan had chosen the ranch. "I made that drive three times since I left this morning just to check on these guys." Belle could see the longing on Ivy's face as she petted Imogene. A child, especially an only child, needed that companionship and the chance to experience an animal's love. But she had to give Harlan some credit. At least he wasn't leaving a dog outside during the frigid Montana winters, or allowing one to run free to terrorize neighboring farms. He had made a responsible decision.

"Can I see your piglet?" Ivy asked.

"Would you like to help me get her from the truck?" The girl nodded and Belle immediately noticed the resemblance to Harlan at that age. "Okay, come with me."

"I'm sorry your grandma is sick." Ivy reached for her hand as they walked outside, instantly melting her heart. "And I'm glad my daddy married you to help make it better."

"Thank you." Belle choked down a sob. What was it about this man and his daughter that annihilated any remaining resolve she had left? She didn't dare look back at Harlan. One Slade was more than she could handle at the moment. She opened the passenger-side door and lifted out the carrier. "Do you think you can bring this inside for me while I grab my bags?"

Ivy nodded.

"Hold on tight." The girl's ponytail swayed from side to side as Belle followed her back to the stable.

"Can I help you feed her?" Ivy asked.

"We have to check with your dad first." Belle looked over her shoulder at Harlan. "Is it okay if she comes upstairs with me?"

He quickly tugged his hat down to shield his glassy eyes and nodded wordlessly. Belle's first instinct was to go to him, but she thought better of it. The man deserved his privacy. It couldn't be easy seeing another woman with his daughter on their ranch. She could only hope Molly had a good reason for leaving Ivy the way she had. She'd hoped the same for her own mother. At least Molly had the good sense to leave her daughter with a responsible adult. Someday Ivy would realize that fact alone counted for something. Belle hadn't been so lucky. She'd found no trace of her mother... alive or dead. And maybe it was for the best. The reality that she was the last surviving member of her family smacked her in the face every time she visited her grandmother. And it hurt. It really hurt.

"Don't be sad." Ivy hugged her around the waist.

"I'm okay, sweetie." Belle instinctively hugged her in return. So this was what Harlan's daughter was like. It had taken her all of two seconds to fall in love with the child. And that meant trouble. Trouble for Belle and what was left of her heart. "Let's go feed Lillie."

Ivy climbed the stairs as Belle picked up the small carrier. She glanced in Harlan's direction, but his back remained to her. She followed her pint-size assistant to the makeshift kitchenette area of the studio apartment. Ivy chatted happily to Lillie while Belle mixed up more formula. She filled an oral syringe and grabbed a towel before joining Ivy in the middle of the floor. The piglet began to push on the front of her carrier door in anticipation of her next meal. It was one more positive sign she'd make a full recovery.

"Here, let's cover your lap." Belle spread the faded blue terry-cloth towel she'd brought from her old apartment across Ivy. "She's wiggly. And you have to be careful of the sunburn on her back. Are you ready?"

Ivy's enthusiastic nod and wide toothless smile warmed her soul. This was how a child should grow up. She'd only been a year younger than Ivy when her mother abandoned her in that terrifying hotel. For years, she had wondered what she'd done wrong to make her mother leave. Sometime in her early teens she realized it hadn't been her fault. While that epiphany had been freeing, the damage had already been done. She'd learned not to trust at such an early age that she'd struggled with it her entire life. Belle wanted to shield Ivy from that pain and privately vowed to remain the child's friend and protector long after her marriage to Harlan ended.

"I can't even feel her on me," Ivy said as Lillie circled on top of the towel.

"She's extremely underweight." Belle placed the syringe in Ivy's hand. "You hold it close enough for her to reach it and I'll push the plunger so she can eat."

"Okay." Ivy cradled the piglet's backside and held the syringe in front of Lillie's mouth. "Eat it all up so you can get big and strong."

Belle laughed. "When she grows up, she will probably weigh over six hundred pounds."

"Really?" Ivy's jaw dropped. "How much do my daddy's horses weigh?"

"Almost double that."

"That's a big pig. Will she stay here with you?"

Belle winced. Ivy had already decided she was staying with them long term. Maybe she wasn't too far off. If Harlan gave her the acreage he'd promised for the rescue, then she'd be on the other side of the ranch.

"Unless I find a safe forever home for Lillie, she'll stay with me."

"Will you teach me how to take care of the animals?" Ivy asked.

"Sure, unless your daddy says otherwise."

"He won't." Ivy lifted her chin. "I already told him I want to be a veterinarian when I grow up. He promised to make it happen."

How had she been lucky enough to befriend a child with her same passions? Maybe it wasn't such an anomaly. Both Harlan and Molly had been her best friends. It stood to reason their daughter inherited their positive traits.

"I'll do whatever I can to help you make that dream happen, too."

There it was again…her commitment to a child she'd just met. Harlan's child. And being around her meant being around him. Indefinitely. Belle never believed she'd ever warm to that idea, but somewhere between the wedding and Ivy, she'd let go of the anger. And it felt good. Maybe forgiveness wasn't as impossible as she'd once thought.

HARLAN HADN'T INTENDED to take Outlaw for a ride, but after seeing Belle with his daughter, he needed to clear his head. He tightened the saddle's cinch strap and mounted the horse. Halfway down the ranch road he realized he should have asked Belle if she would mind watching Ivy. He trusted her with his child. That alone bothered him, but not like he thought it would. The two had taken to each other much quicker and smoother than he'd expected. His daughter's desperation for a mother just collided with Belle's desire for a family, and the outcome—at least from where he stood—felt right. As if Belle was finally home.

But it wasn't her home. Ivy wasn't her daughter and Harlan once again feared he would hurt the two people he loved more than anything in this world. He nudged his horse into a run once they reached open land. The animal's powerful muscles flexed under the weight of his body, giving Harlan the much-needed strength to make the best decisions for his family. And he wanted that family to include Belle even though he had no right to that desire.

Harlan walked Outlaw back to the ranch, allowing the horse to cool down. Once they reached the stables, he removed the tack and filled the trough with fresh water. When Outlaw finished drinking, Harlan hosed the animal off, then walked him on the shaded side of the stables. The sun didn't set behind the Mission Mountains until nine this time of year and it almost always produced a spectacular display. The colors were equally gorgeous when the sun rose over the Swan Range every morning. He'd never tire of the views from his ranch. He was just tired of watching them alone.

Ivy bounded down the stable stairs with Belle in tow. "I fed Lillie, Daddy!" She animatedly danced in front of him. "She's so cute. But she has a blister on her back and Belle said I can help take care of her."

Harlan smiled at Belle in acknowledgment before turning his attention to Ivy. "Go clean up for dinner. I made chili. I'll be there in a minute."

"Can Belle eat with us?" Ivy reached for both of their hands and swung them back and forth.

"Honey, Belle doesn't eat meat," Harlan said. "It wouldn't be fair for her to sit and watch us."

"I don't mind eating with you. I picked up a salad on the way home."

"Then we'd love to have you join us."

Belle laughed. "Remember when we were kids? You'd order a burger, and I'd eat all your fries."

"She sure did," Harlan said to Ivy. "I went years without ever tasting a French fry."

"I wasn't that bad." She playfully swatted at him.

"Yeah, you were." His heart warmed as they shared a smile for the first time in years. "Come over when ever you're ready. Afterward, we'll pick up the rest of your stuff from your apartment."

"Calvin—Lydia's husband—already did earlier. I hope that was okay."

"That's fine. Calvin's a good man and he, Lydia and the kids are welcome here anytime they want."

"I'll let them know. Give me twenty minutes, okay? I need to clean up."

"Sounds good." Harlan ran up the back porch steps

behind Ivy. He gave the house a quick going-over before he set the table. He looked around, satisfied. It was clean and reasonably organized, at least by single-dad standards.

He scanned the living room and mentally prepared himself to welcome Belle. Last night he hadn't given it a second thought until she opted to stay in the apartment above the stables. Then the realization had dawned on him. It had to be difficult for her to come into what should have been their home after everything he'd put her through.

Once Molly had left, he redecorated the house the way he and Belle had planned. It wasn't perfect. Far from it, but it was still a work in progress. Ivy added her own frilly additions, but the place could stand a woman's touch. He wasn't sure if Belle had a change of heart because Ivy had forced the issue or if her curiosity had gotten the best of her. Now he wondered if it had been such a good idea. Not for her sake, but for his own.

A soft rap emanated from the porch screen door. He ran his palms down the front of his Wranglers and noticed he still had on his uniform shirt. He wished he'd changed out of it before she arrived.

"I'll get it." Ivy ran past him to the door. "Belle's here!" his daughter shouted at the top of her lungs.

"I can see that." Harlan joined them in the kitchen and lightly tugged Ivy's ponytail. "No need to yell, sweetheart."

"Want to see my room?" Ivy dragged Belle across the kitchen without waiting for an answer.

"Don't be rude, Ivy," Harlan warned. "Belle hasn't even put her salad down."

"I feel bad not bringing anything. Like a yummy rich dessert." She reached down and tickled his daughter, immediately lightening the mood again. "Next time, huh, kiddo?" Belle straightened. "That is if there is a next time. I don't want to intrude."

"You're not intruding. Remember what I told you last night. You're more than welcome to—" Harlan hadn't had the pleasure of talking to a woman he was attracted to around his daughter before. He was learning to be more careful with his words. "Would you like a glass of wine? I have a sparkling white and a merlot."

"The white would be wonderful, thank you."

"Your ring matches Daddy's." Ivy lifted Belle's hand and fiddled with the gold band.

"I thought—"

"In case I—"

Harlan and Belle both spoke at the same time.

"I'm sorry, go ahead," Harlan said, praying his daughter would stop putting them on the spot tonight.

Belle's cheeks flushed. "It was easier to leave it on so I don't have to remember it every time I visit my grandmother."

"Me, too," he lied. The fact she cared enough to save the rings made him want to wear it. "I figured there would be fewer questions around town since everyone seems to know we got married. Turns out it was more of a conversation starter, but I handled it."

"I hate that you're going through this because of me. I deal little with the public and most of the animals don't pay too much attention to my jewelry."

Harlan poured Belle a glass of wine and handed it to her. He opened his mouth to speak, when he realized they still had an audience. "Why don't you go sit down, Ivy?" He pulled out a chair for Belle before spooning the chili into bowls for him and his daughter. He joined them at the table and reached for both of their hands. "Thank You, Lord, for these blessings which we are about to receive. And thank You for bringing Belle, along with her fine-feathered and four-legged friends, into our lives." Ivy giggled. "Please watch over and bless us all. In Jesus's name. Amen."

"Amen." Belle gave his hand a light squeeze before releasing it. "It's nice to see things haven't changed."

Harlan longed for the physical contact as soon as she let go. As much as he'd told himself they had both moved on and couldn't be together again, having a meal together as a family made him wonder if it was possible.

Dinner had gone remarkably well. He couldn't remember the last time he'd seen his daughter laugh so much. A little too much, considering she wore a good portion of her chili. Ivy surprised him when she asked Belle to read her a story instead of him. But Belle didn't hesitate to say yes and seemed touched by the request. While they were upstairs, he wondered if Belle felt uncomfortable being in the room they had chosen for their own children. He wanted to ask her when she came back downstairs and joined him on the couch, but he didn't want to ruin an otherwise perfect evening.

"I can't thank you enough for having me. I had a wonderful time." Belle rested her hand on his forearm. "And I mean that. Your daughter is amazing. You should be very proud."

"I should be the one saying thanks. I think you won her over." A warning voice grew in his head.

Belle withdrew from him. "And that bothers you, doesn't it?"

"Yes, it does." Harlan turned sideways and draped one arm over the back of the couch so he could face her. "She gets very attached to people. She doesn't have a lot of family outside of my uncle Jax and my brothers Dylan and Wes, when Wes is even around. He's stayed away since Dad's death. Ivy doesn't remember Molly. And that's a good thing. Sad but good. She only has two cousins—my brother Garrett's kids— but once Mom moved to California he stopped coming back to town."

"She doesn't see Molly's family?"

Harlan scrubbed his hand along his jawline. "They've made no effort to see Ivy. And they know she exists because we sent them a birth announcement. I had tried to contact them after Molly left. Never heard a word. I've made peace with it. This way I don't have to worry about them disappointing my daughter. It's sad she doesn't have more family, though. I grew up with four brothers and chaos everywhere. And as crazy as my family was, I wouldn't have traded them in for anything. It kills me sometimes. I always wanted a couple of kids growing up together. Ivy will never experience that bond of having a sibling close in age."

"I know what you mean." A bittersweet hint of emotion filled her voice.

"I'm such an ass." Guilt rolled through him. "Here

I am rambling on about raising another woman's child without even considering how difficult this must be for you. And I know you don't want to hear this and I don't want to ruin a nice evening, but you need to know the truth. That one night with Molly was all it ever was. One night. A drunken mistake that resulted in the most beautiful gift. But we were never together again. I never meant to hurt you. Not then and not now. Yet I keep doing it, don't I?"

"You're giving yourself too much credit." A cool detachment replaced any sentiment he sensed a moment ago. "I'll admit it was difficult coming into this house and seeing it as I had always envisioned it, but none of this hurts me. You moved on with your life and so have I."

"Everything around here is mine and Ivy's. The paint color, the furnishings. I changed it all after Molly left."

"You don't owe me an explanation." Belle rose from the couch, crossed the room to the fireplace and admired the photos of his family on the mantel. "This is your home and I respect that. Things didn't work out and, honestly, I'm exhausted from holding it against you." She faced him, her expression softened. "I'm exhausted from hating you for it. And yes, *hate* is a strong word and I felt that way for a long time. Over the past couple of days, I discovered the beauty of letting go. I didn't even realize I had done it until Ivy and I were feeding Lillie."

Harlan perched on the edge of the couch and rested his elbows on his knees. Was she saying they had a chance? "What made you change your mind?"

"It just clicked." She shrugged. "I enjoy spending time with you and Ivy. I didn't know what to expect when I walked in. Seeing the house wasn't as bad as I thought it would be." Belle held up her hands in front of her. "Before you ask me again, no, I will not move in here with you. I think that will confuse matters even more. I understand your concerns with Ivy getting too attached. Providing you keep up your word on the land deal, I don't see myself walking out of her life anytime soon. Once the rescue is open, I'll just be on the other side of the ranch and she can visit me whenever she wants."

Belle's willingness to be a part of Ivy's life erased any lingering doubts he had about offering her the acreage. "I admit, your attitude surprises me."

"Me, too. But how can I promote kindness and compassion toward animals and not give you the same courtesy?" Belle's eyes widened. "Not that I'm calling you an animal, because I'm not."

Harlan laughed. "I wondered there for a second."

Belle sat next to him again on the couch. "This is good. You and I have finally reached the point where we can laugh with one another even if it's at the other's expense. Who knows what the future holds, but I think we can be friends if you're okay with that?"

"Yes, I'm okay with that." He'd much rather take her in his arms and tell her exactly how she made him feel and that he wanted to be more than friends, but he couldn't. It wasn't worth the risk of driving her away. He'd missed her infectious laughter and being able to share things that happened in his life or even throughout the day. Especially when his father had died. That was when he had needed her most. Nobody understood him the way she always had. And even though they weren't together, he'd had a sense of calm and relief when he saw her at the cemetery. No words had been necessary. He'd felt her concern and sympathy. He refused to let her slip away from him again. If friendship was all they'd ever have, he'd take it. But he wouldn't lose her again.

"I need to give Lillie her next feeding." Belle stood. "Thank you again for having me over tonight."

Harlan led her through the kitchen and once again found himself unsure how to say good-night. He opened the door. "Could we do this again tomorrow?"

"Can we play it by ear?" Belle nibbled her lower lip. "My schedule is all over the place between my grandmother and veterinary emergencies. It makes it a little difficult to plan anything. I would like to, though."

"I'll take that as a yes and if you get tied up, then don't give it a second thought. I understand the call of duty. I've had to drop Ivy off at my uncle's house on numerous occasions."

"It's a date, then." Belle's mouth dropped open. "I didn't mean a date. I meant—"

"I know what you meant." Harlan wished it was a date. "I wouldn't be much of a gentleman if I didn't offer to walk you back to your apartment."

She laughed. "It's only a few feet away. I can manage." Belle stepped onto the porch. "Wow, that sunset is stunning. I forgot the view from here. You're blessed to see this every day."

Harlan joined her at the porch railing. "You're living here, too. It's your view just as much as it's mine."

"I can't live above the stables forever."

"You and the animals are welcome as long as you want." Harlan already hated the thought of her leaving. "You are still planning on living here until the rescue center's built, right?"

"Construction is still a long way off. I don't think you want me around that long. Maybe I'll put a travel trailer out there once I get everything operational. It's an inexpensive, although a temporary, solution. I probably wouldn't survive the winter in one. Maybe a prefabricated home somewhere down the line. I need to focus on donations to make this happen. I can't use that money for myself. And I'm still not sure how I'll balance working for Lydia and running the rescue. But I need an income. And I'll need plenty of volunteers along with paid employees. I feel guilty taking a salary for myself. Eventually, I'll have to get over it, but there's a lot I still have to work out. I am so grateful to you for the land."

"No need to thank me." Harlan laughed, amazed at how fast and long she could talk without coming up for air. He could stand on the porch and listen to her all night.

"I know, I know. I'm rambling." She sheepishly looked away.

Harlan lifted her chin with his finger. "You're excited and rightfully so. Enjoy it."

She nodded, and in that moment he wanted nothing more than to kiss her.

"I guess I should feed my little ones."

Harlan chuckled at her timing. "Yes, you definitely should. I need to check on Ivy."

"Thanks again for tonight." Belle reached up and kissed him on the cheek before darting down the porch steps toward the stables.

The sweet gesture sent his pulse racing once again. And he loved every second. Maybe there was hope for them after all.

Chapter Six

Belle woke up giggling. The sound startled her at first until she realized it was her own laughter. She sat up in bed and giggled again. And then she laughed out loud. She was actually happy. It had been a rarity in recent years. So rare she couldn't remember the last time she had been in such a good mood.

She reached over the bed and checked on Lillie in her carrier. The tiny piglet was awake and standing at the door. It was another great sign. She opened the door and scooped her up with one hand, holding her close to her chest.

"Good morning, sweet thing." Lillie wiggled excitedly in her arms. "I can't tell you how glad I am to see you moving around on your own. I guess we both slept well."

She climbed out of bed and slipped a small collar around Lillie's neck. "Let's take you outside to go potty before breakfast." It may be August but the morning air was chilly. Belle bounced up and down to stay warm. She'd started leash training Lillie yesterday at work and so far the piglet didn't seem to mind it. "Hurry up before you freeze your tail off." After ten minutes of sniffing around, she went to the bathroom. "Good girl."

The sound of a twig snapping nearby startled them both. A puff of steam four feet off the ground appeared from the corner of the stables. Belle picked Lillie up and stuffed her in her shirt before plastering herself against the wood siding. She couldn't run, for fear whatever it was would chase after them. She held her breath as a moose and her calf appeared. The cow looked in her direction, then continued walking toward the corral and along the fence. Her calf didn't follow and Belle was afraid it would pick up her scent and come in for a closer look.

Moose were larger than most people thought, weighing between eight hundred and twelve hundred pounds. Thankfully, this female was on the small end. Belle had been up close and personal with one only once and that was when she and Lydia had rescued a bull moose caught in a barbed-wire fence a few years ago. It had been one of their most difficult rescues due to the animal's size and strength.

Lillie squirmed and Belle prayed she wouldn't squeal. The calf finally lost interest and followed her mother. When they were a safe enough distance away, Belle inched along the stable's outer wall, never taking her eyes off the moose. When she reached the corner, she peered around it to make sure there weren't any more. Once she was inside, she breathed a sigh of relief and eased Lillie out from under her shirt.

"That was enough adventure for one day, wasn't it, little girl?"

She looked toward the corridor to see if the animals

had sensed any trouble. Horses were usually the most intuitive and would sometimes bang against their stalls or use the flehmen response, where they curled back their upper lip, exposed their teeth and inhaled with their nostrils closed in an attempt to identify a scent.

Assured all was quiet, she climbed the stairs and continued with her morning. After she fed Lillie, swaddled her and put her down for a nap, Belle showered and changed into her work clothes, then headed back down to the stables. She couldn't seem to get warm. The thermometer outside the door read thirty-nine degrees. "Holy crap!" No wonder she was cold. Yesterday morning had been closer to sixty.

She opened Samson's stall and picked up the black lamb. She rubbed her face against his head, relishing the feel of the soft fleece against her skin. The always jealous Olive butted her head against the neighboring stall, wanting affection of her own. Belle reached over the side and scratched her back. "Be patient. You'll get yours. There is enough love to go around." Imogene honked at her from behind Olive. "Yes, I love you, too."

The stable door slid open and Harlan appeared, silhouetted by the morning sun. There was nothing sexier than a cowboy first thing in the morning. She'd denied herself the pleasure of his piercing blue eyes and slow, easy smile yesterday morning. She wouldn't make the same mistake today. Besides, the wedding ring on her finger entitled her to that enjoyment, and she deserved to partake in at least some of it. Looking was harmless, right?

"Good morning." Harlan handed her a cup of coffee over the stall door. "Looks like I got here before you started mucking. Good. Now I won't have to argue with you about it."

Belle lowered Samson into the fluffy pile of hay and sipped her coffee. "Thank you. I needed this."

"It's a cold one."

"Well, that too, but that's not the only reason I need an extra pick-me-up. Lillie and I had a run-in with a mama moose and her calf."

"Really?" He stopped midsip. "They haven't been around the ranch in a few years. I'll buy some moose deterrent in town later. Are you two all right?"

"We're fine." Belle checked the time on her phone. "Remember back in high school when that bull moose attacked the principal's car in the middle of the day?"

"I forgot about that. Poor creature thought he'd found the love of his life." Harlan laughed. "And we had to stay inside until the police came and chased him away. Good times."

Belle almost snorted her coffee. "Yes, they were." Once again she found herself easily laughing with Harlan. A part of her wanted to warn her inner self to be careful. It would be far too easy to fall for him only to end up heartbroken. They had both agreed the marriage was temporary and it needed to stay that way. Belle finally had a chance at fulfilling her dream and she wouldn't allow her feelings for Harlan to confuse the issue. The last thing she needed or wanted was for a romantic relationship—however brief—to destroy his promise to donate his land to the rescue. The animals needed her more than she needed him.

"Hey, since I'm probably closer during the day, do you want me to swing by and feed Samson later?"

"Harlan Slade!" Belle closed the stall door and joined him in the stable corridor. "You won't stop home during the day so your daughter can have a dog, but you'll do it for my lamb?"

Harlan grimaced. "True. Ivy would never let me live it down."

"Hang your head in shame," Belle teased. "It's no secret I believe in the adopt, don't shop mentality, but I know of a litter of blue heelers, and every puppy deserves a good home."

"I can't believe you remembered."

"You talked about it for a year straight. Said once we got married you'd get one and name him Elvis." Belle wondered why Harlan hadn't gone through with his plan after marrying Molly. "Surprise! We're married."

"Who has the litter?" Harlan rubbed his jawline, causing Belle to wonder if his face was still as soft as it used to be right after he shaved.

"One of Lydia's clients. If you're interested, I'll call him. I have to stop in here during the day anyway, so I can help out with puppy training. And once I'm next door, it won't be any hardship to check in on him while you're at work." The words sounded more real each time she said them aloud. She never would have thought she'd live on the ranch they picked out together.

"You'd do that for me?"

"Not for you—for both of you. Last night when I was reading to Ivy, she told me how much she wants a dog. The companionship is good for an only child."

Harlan nodded. "Okay, yeah, make the call and let me know how much."

"Will do." Belle planned to give the puppy to Harlan and Ivy in exchange for allowing her to stay on the ranch. Once Ivy had the puppy in her hands, then she'd tell him it was a gift. He wouldn't be able to argue with her then.

She realized it was dangerous to be making so many long-term plans with the man she'd only started talking to again a few days ago, but it felt right. If she maintained an emotional distance, everything would work out fine.

"Ivy, meet Elvis. He's all yours." Belle held out a blue-and-gray-speckled puppy with tan markings to Ivy. "He's a blue heeler, also known as an Australian cattle dog."

"Really?" Ivy looked from Belle to Harlan before taking the dog. "We can keep him, Daddy?"

"Yes, sweetheart. He's ours."

"Thank you." Ivy hugged the dog close to her chest as tears streamed down her cheeks. "Thank you, so much."

The look on his daughter's face took his breath away. She was a happy child, but not necessarily an expressive one. She'd learned to compartmentalize her feelings at an early age. At least, that's what the therapist had told him. Today was different. Just as it had been after Ivy fed Lillie for the first time. He hated to admit it, but Belle brought out the best in his daughter. Not that there was anything wrong with that, except it put his emotions on the line even more than they already were.

Harlan sat down next to Ivy on the living room floor. "Honey, if you cry, you'll get your dog all wet." But

Elvis had already licked her tears dry. "He's perfect." He turned to Belle. "Thank you for getting him. How much do I owe you?" He began to pull out his wallet before Belle stilled his hand.

"You don't." She knelt beside him. "And please don't sneak the money to me by hiding it somewhere in my things. This is my gift. I need to do this."

Belle didn't have a dollar to spare, let alone the hundreds the puppy must have cost her. While he was grateful for the gift, he didn't want her going into debt because of his daughter.

"This will be hard to beat at Christmas." Harlan wondered if Belle would still be living on the ranch when the holidays rolled around. While the stables were heated, the upstairs apartment never got above sixty degrees in the winter because the sun wasn't strong enough to heat the building that time of year. He'd insist on her moving into the house once the first snow fell. The idea of spending Christmas with Belle excited him more than he thought possible. He wasn't sure who would be more delighted. Him or his daughter.

"I suggest you start talking to Santa's elves now."

"What will you ask Santa for this year?" Harlan teased.

"Peace for my grandmother." Belle scooted back to rest against the front of the couch. "In whatever form that may come. I don't even know if she'll still be around at Christmas."

"Did you see her today?" Harlan joined her, giving Ivy more room to roll around on the floor with Elvis.

"Twice. She's always good in the morning. She recognized me and still remembered our wedding. She even asked about you. When I went to see her this afternoon, she was confused and didn't know where she was. Most of the time she thinks she's in the hospital for various reasons. You saw it. Earlier this week she believed she was there for her hip. When she gets like that, it usually means another chunk of her memory is disappearing. Tomorrow she may drift further back in time. I'm scared at her rate of regression this month."

"I'll stop in and visit with her tomorrow during lunch." Harlan wrapped his arm around Belle's shoulder and pulled her close. He didn't care if it wasn't part of their arrangement or worry he might push her away. Right now they were a family—however unconventional—and she deserved comfort from a friend.

She didn't resist. Instead, she laid her head on his shoulder and they watched Ivy play. Until the puppy bounded for Belle's bare, painted toes and took a tiny nip.

"Hey, those are mine." Belle tucked her legs, shifting her body closer to Harlan's. The puppy barked and attempted to squeeze between her and the couch. "I'm not candy." Belle laughed and screeched as she tried to climb over Harlan's lap before landing in the middle of it when Elvis nipped at her behind. Harlan wrapped his arms around her tight as she scooped up the puppy, flipped him on his back across her legs and tickled his chubby belly. The house filled with laughter for the first time in eight years. And it was the best sound he'd ever heard.

ALMOST A WEEK and a half had passed since their wedding day. Despite only seeing each other for an hour or two in the evenings, if they were lucky, the three of them had managed to eat dinner every night together. Belle and Harlan had developed a comfortable little routine, filling in for the other when work called them away. He and Ivy now spoke fluent baby animal. Earlier tonight, Lydia had brought Belle out on an emergency call shortly after they'd finished eating. Then one of the deputies had phoned in sick and he needed to cover half of the shift.

Harlan drove away from Dylan's house after dropping off Ivy and her puppy. He hated being on patrol. It took him all over the county and too far away from Ivy. Although, he never had to worry when she was with his brother. Dylan doted on her as if she were his own. His brother's ex-wife took off with his two stepkids after he'd partnered with their uncle Jax on the Silver Bells Ranch almost five years ago. She wanted no part of ranch life and Dylan couldn't convince her otherwise. He had loved those kids more than life itself and had been devastated after they left. During that time, Ivy became a real comfort to him.

Harlan just wished he and his brother had more to talk about than Ivy. Dylan had accused Harlan of siding with Ryder after their father's death. Considering Ryder pled guilty and the case never went to trial, there were no sides to take. But Dylan hadn't seen it that way and in some respects, he'd been right.

Having been the first to arrive on the scene that night, Harlan had a gut instinct something was off. He knew Ryder. And he knew what Ryder was like when he was drunk. And that night, Ryder hadn't been drunk enough to accidentally kill their father. But that's what he had confessed in his statement. None of that mattered anymore. It was in the past and he wanted to move forward for his and his daughter's sake. He'd give just about anything to see his family together again.

His cell phone rang. A photo of Belle in her wedding dress, courtesy of his uncle Jax, lit the screen. "Hello. Heading home?"

"Not exactly."

Harlan steered his police cruiser onto the shoulder and turned on the lights for safety. Two words in and he already didn't like the sound of Belle's voice. "What happened?"

"Do you know where the Huffington cattle ranch is?"

"Mmm-hmm. I do." Harlan's jaw pulsated. "What did you do?"

"Nothing." A muffled sound came from the phone. Harlan only made out his own name. "You said to call before I broke any laws. Lydia and I both need you. We were on an emergency call when we saw a yearling with what appeared to be a broken leg. When we got closer, Lydia realized the leg is almost severed below the carpal joint. The wound is fresh. He must have caught it on something. The animal needs to be either put down humanely or brought in for surgery. Lydia's already contacted a large-animal vet in Kalispell and they will take him. But the owner won't release him to us. We need your help. This bull is suffering."

Harlan rubbed his eye with the palm of his hand.

"I'm on patrol on the other side of the county. I'll call it in and see if someone closer can get over there."

"Whoa, wait a minute." Belle's voice pitched. "If someone can get here? There's no if, Harlan. The law states failure to provide medical care to a severely injured animal comes under animal cruelty."

"Poor choice of words on my part. Yes, it is considered alleged animal cruelty. I will get someone over there and I'll try to get there, too. Promise me you won't do anything."

"Just hurry, Harlan." Belle's voice sounded defeated as she hung up the phone.

"Shit." Harlan smacked the steering wheel. He made a U-turn and drove toward the Huffington ranch before something bad happened.

"You can't keep me here against my will." Belle held her hands in the air. She had no idea if someone had a gun aimed at her, but she wasn't taking any chances. She felt like a deer in the headlights. And that's exactly what she was. Caught in the headlights by high-powered floodlights mounted on top of the many trucks that now surrounded her within the confines of the Huffington cattle ranch. She only hoped she'd provided enough of a diversion for Lydia and her husband to get away unnoticed. "This is kidnapping."

"You're trespassing," a voice said from the darkness. "The sheriff's department is on the way."

Oh, Lord. She tried to imagine how Harlan would react when he heard the news. In all fairness, she'd called him, but after four hours they had to intervene before the young bull died.

"Good, I'm glad the sheriff is coming. Then he can arrest you for animal cruelty. If you had allowed us to treat the bull, we would have been on our way." Belle's legs shook, betraying the calm demeanor she attempted to convey. "And don't even think about destroying that animal before they get here. I took photos and video and already uploaded it to the cloud, so don't get any bright ideas about taking my phone either."

"Our herd is none of your business," another voice said.

That did it. "The hell it's not." Belle lowered her arms and stormed toward the voice. No one would bully her into kowtowing to a bunch of wannabe renegades. She followed the sound of the man's laughter until she broke through the floodlight line and finally got a good look at his face. He stood on the bed of a pickup, all big and bad. Okay, so he did appear somewhat menacing up there. "Just because this is private property doesn't mean you can do whatever you want. There are laws and you're breaking them."

"So are you." The man jumped over the side of the truck's bed and landed inches in front of her. The smell of chewing tobacco and sweat offended her nostrils.

"Personal space." Belle thrust her arms forward. "You don't intimidate me. I'm protecting that bull's well-being. You're just cruel. You won't do a damn thing because you don't want to lose the money from one head of cattle. That's pathetic. Do you even own this place or are you just the hired muscle?"

"Belle, enough!" Harlan's voice boomed. "Sheriff's department. Turn off all those floodlights and cut the engines on the trucks. Now!"

"Someone mind telling me what is going on here?" Sheriff Parker demanded.

Before Belle could answer, Harlan gripped her arm and led her away from the circle of the vehicles. "I told you to wait."

"I waited four hours." Belle pulled from his grasp. "No one came."

"I had to respond to an accident along the way. I have a job to do."

"And so do I." How dare he think his job was more important than hers? She deserved just as much respect. "You could have called and told me, but you didn't. You said someone would come out, and they didn't. I promised to call you first. I did everything you asked. It accomplished nothing."

Harlan tilted his hat back, his expression softening slightly. "Tell me what happened."

Belle explained her and Lydia's plan to take the bull when they found him standing alone in the pastures. At least the Huffington ranch raised grass-fed cattle and wasn't a jam-packed feedlot. Lydia had remained with the bull while Calvin attempted to reason with the ranch's owner. In the meantime, Belle had driven back to the ranch, borrowed Harlan's trailer and returned. That's when she spotted the ranch trucks barreling toward Lydia. Belle drove straight into the foray, giving her friends a chance to escape.

"Where is the bull now?"

"That's a good question. I warned them that nothing better happen to that animal. I have video."

"Show it to me, please."

Belle handed Harlan her phone. "Look here, the

lower half of that front leg is barely attached." She looked up and saw concern and disgust in Harlan's eyes. The urgency had finally registered. "He left a blood trail before—I'm sure we can find it again, provided a wolf or a coyote hasn't gotten to him already."

"Show me where you last saw him." Harlan sent the video to his phone before handing it back to her.

Within twenty minutes, they located the injured bull. Harlan didn't say a word at the sight of the animal. He pressed a button on the side of his police radio hand mic attached to the front of his shirt. "Officer 19, I found the injured bull. He's in need of immediate medical attention. Requesting authorization to contact Dr. Lydia Presley."

"Ten-four," Sheriff Parker responded.

"Sheriff, you need to come see this."

After Lydia and Calvin returned with her truck and trailer, they loaded the bull for the short ride to the large-animal hospital in Kalispell. They promised to call her once they knew more. Belle checked her phone. She'd started the stopwatch when she first called Harlan. Almost seven hours later and the bull was getting the care it needed. Hopefully they weren't too late. It never should have gone on this long. Belle debated whether she would bother calling Harlan in the future. They had lost so much time.

"Harlan, I think you need to come up here," Bryan called him on the radio.

His jaw tensed as they walked toward Belle's pickup. There was his horse trailer hooked to the back of it. "You planned on stealing a bull with my trailer?" Harlan spun to face her. "I work for the sheriff's department! How do you think this reflects back on me when one of my vehicles is involved in a theft?"

"Your ranch was closer than Lydia's and we didn't have time."

"Yet here we are, hours later, and Lydia just left with the bull."

"I made a judgment call. You told me you probably would have done the same thing."

"After I notified the station. I should arrest you and let you spend the night in jail just on principle."

Belle didn't appreciate getting chewed out in front of half the police department and the men who had tried to intimidate her hours earlier. How could someone be compassionate and understanding one minute and a total jerk the next?

"You need to worry about arresting them, not me."

"And they will be. Maybe I'll put you in the adjoining cell." The vein on the side of his forehead twitched and Belle sensed his annoyance was real.

"It can't be worse than leaving me at the altar." Belle fumed. "Besides, I have animals to take care of at home."

"Ivy and I will take care of them. I'm sure Lydia will explain exactly what we need to do." Harlan removed the cuffs from his belt. "Belle Barnes—correction, Slade—you're under arrest for the theft of my trailer. You have the right to remain—"

"You've got to be kidding me!" The cold steel encircled her wrists. "And it's still Barnes. I didn't take your last name."

"—silent. Anything you say can and will be used against you in a court of law. You have the right to an attorney. If you cannot afford an attorney, one will be provided for you. Do you understand these rights I have just read to you?"

"Is it even legal for you to arrest your own wife?" Belle tried to squeeze her hands out of the cuffs.

"I can and I just did." Harlan led her to his police cruiser and opened the door. "Look where we are again. Watch your head."

He slammed the door and left her there for the next half hour. So much for today's happiness. Surely, he'd release her as soon as he got back. Harlan wouldn't take her to jail. Would he?

Chapter Seven

"You can't leave her in there," Bryan said. "Judge Sanders will have your badge for tying up his courtroom over this. Technically, she can say the trailer was community property and she had every right to use it."

"She doesn't know that. Let her stew in there for a little while longer. Her heart was in the right place, but if she had gotten away with taking that bull and someone reported the plates on my trailer, I'd have more than one problem on my hands." Harlan watched her cell on the monitor. "She'll survive another hour."

"Harlan," Sheriff Bill Parker called to him across the station. "My office."

"Here we go." Harlan trudged down the hall.

"Have a seat." Bill closed the door behind him. "You got married when? August 1, right?"

Harlan nodded.

"And what time is it now?" The older man glanced at the clock on the wall. "Five after midnight on Friday. So, you haven't even been married for ten and a half days, give or take a few hours. Am I right?"

Harlan groaned. Their conversation was headed in the direction he'd hope to avoid. "Yes, you're correct."

"Then can you please explain why your wife has been arrested twice during that time?"

"Well, sir—"

"We all agreed to drop the trespassing charge due to the animal cruelty charges against the Huffington cattle ranch. And for the record, I know your wife's employer was a part of all of this, but I overlooked it to keep the peace in your family. And can you also explain why you arrested Belle for the theft of marital property?"

"I wanted to teach her a lesson. It's not a real arrest. I wanted her to think it was, though. I'll release her soon."

Bill placed both hands and his desk and leaned over it. "You'll release her before this goes any further than this department."

"Yes, sir. Should I do it right this second?"

Bill straightened. "Harlan, get out of my office!"

He scrambled for the door. He hadn't heard the sheriff yell at anyone since a rookie drove their cruiser into the Swan River. He grabbed Belle's personal belongings from his desk, swiped his key card and entered the holding cells. Belle sat on a bench, with a half smile plastered across her face. He'd planned on letting her out once the Huffington gang was through with booking.

"Voices carry around here at night." There was no disguising her grin. She knew he'd gotten reamed out for his prank. "Serves you right."

Harlan unlocked her door and crooked his finger at her. "Come here."

Belle remained seated, her eyes wide. "No, thanks. I'm good."

"Oh, no, you're not. I'm going home and you're coming with me."

"I need to get my truck and your trailer."

"Already taken care of. I had your truck parked in the impound lot for safekeeping overnight. You can get it tomorrow."

"Thanks a lot, Harlan. I didn't even deserve to get arrested and now I have to pay for my truck. You're a real prize of a husband." She grabbed the bag from his hands and pushed past him, waiting for him to unlock the holding area doors.

"You don't have to pay to pick up your truck tomorrow. It's just there for the night."

"Fine."

"Fine."

They stood in the hallway facing each other. "If you don't mind, I have little ones at home to feed."

"After you." Harlan swept his hand to the side. "Come on. Admit it. I got you good that time."

Belle's hand froze on the doorknob. "I'm tired of you getting me." She faced him. "I'm tired of being a joke. Your joke."

"I thought we were past all of that."

"So did I." She turned away. "I guess your plan backfired. It gave me time to think."

"Wait." Harlan reached for her, feeling her body stiffen beneath his touch. "I'm sorry. I shouldn't have arrested you tonight." He held her face gently. "You did everything I had asked and I failed you. I should have called and given you an update when I knew I couldn't get there. I should have tried harder, and I didn't."

"Harlan." Her eyes fluttered closed. She had no idea how sensuous she sounded when she said his name.

Her moistened lips begged for him to taste them. To apologize properly and kiss them the way a man should kiss his wife. His mouth covered hers. He fought to maintain control, but the fervent need to claim her overtook him. Her lips parted, allowing entry with his tongue. Slow languid strokes in time with her own. Her fingers found his chest and splayed across it. He ached for her touch everywhere. Softly, he broke the kiss and reached behind her to open the door. He planned to make love to his wife tonight and the police station wasn't the place.

DESIRE COILED DEEP within Belle during the silent ride home. Harlan's fingers, strong and firm, entwined with hers. She needed to experience those fingers on her bare skin in the most intimate of places. Tonight she'd allow herself the pleasure of being with the man who drove her utterly mad in the most delicious ways, even though she knew she shouldn't. The chance of reliving the passion they'd once shared was impossible to refuse. To feel his love and tenderness, if only for a few hours.

When his cruiser braked alongside his house, her skin prickled in anticipation. She waited for Harlan to open the passenger door. She took his hand as she stepped out, allowing him to fold her into his embrace. His mouth devoured hers. His thumb grazed her engorged nipple over her shirt, circling and teasing. Belle felt his hardness against her, needing to feel it within her.

She pushed away from him. "Slow down, cowboy." She inhaled the night air. "I have to feed Lillie and Samson first."

Harlan kissed the side of her neck and nibbled at her ear before whispering, "I'll feed Samson. I can't wait much longer."

Belle's body tingled as his lips trailed over her skin, sending shocks straight to her core. He led her inside the stables and continued to press kisses against her neck as she prepared two bottles of formula. She handed him one to take down to Samson while she stayed in the apartment and fed Lillie. The piglet devoured her midnight snack and Belle fixed her fresh bedding before ducking into the bathroom. Between the work, tonight's rescue and jail, she needed a shower before she allowed Harlan to see her naked.

She turned on the faucet, letting the water heat as she slipped out of her clothes. Steam filled the room, engulfing her in luxurious warmth. She opened the shower door as the bathroom door eased open. Harlan, raw and naked as the day he was born, entered the room. His hands sought hers as his lips claimed her bare breasts. Her body arched against him, yearning for more. He guided her under the tepid liquid, allowing it to trickle between them. His fingers caressed her in ways she'd remembered in her dreams. Tonight they belonged to each other. She'd worry about the consequences in the morning.

HOURS LATER, Belle awoke next to Harlan. The light of the moon cast a silvery glow around the room. She stretched. Her body still tingled from the glorious passion she'd experienced numerous times during the night with the only man she'd ever shared a bed with. She lifted the covers, soaking in his nakedness. She could get used to this. But was she able to forgive him enough to move forward together into the future?

Somewhere between jail and home every wrong between them had been righted. They had even gone one step further and consummated their marriage. She wasn't sure they qualified for an annulment after that repeated act. The sudden urge to want to stay married to Harlan unnerved her. She had Ivy to consider and the impact it would have on the child.

Belle slid out of bed and padded to the window, grabbing his shirt along the way. She adored Ivy. More than she ever thought she would. She also wanted children of her own one day. Did Harlan want more kids? She wasn't even sure how to ask that question so soon into the relationship. Then again, it had been anything but conventional so far. Why stop now?

Belle pulled the shirt tight across her chest. The room had chilled dramatically since they had arrived home. When she turned to make sure Lillie was warm enough, she noticed a faint glow at the entrance of the ranch drive. *Were those dashboard lights?* There was a flash of red and then the faint sound of an engine starting. Whoever it was must have stepped on the brakes first.

"Harlan," Belle whispered. She tiptoed across the room, uncertain why she was being quiet. "Harlan." She sat on the side of the bed and lightly shook his hand. "There's someone outside."

"What?" He wrapped his arms around her waist and

pulled her next to him. "It's too early and you have too many clothes on," he murmured. "Take them off so I can make love to you again."

"Harlan, there's a—"

His fingers slipped between her thighs, causing her to cease speaking. Someone most likely got lost. By sunup they'd be gone. Why waste time worrying about a stranger? She shed his shirt and tossed it onto the floor, relishing the feel of his rigid body against hers.

"Do you want more kids?" Belle panted between strokes.

"Yes." Harlan's voice was husky with desire. "Let's practice making babies now." He rolled her onto her back and he eased himself on top of her. "There's nothing I'd love more than raising a family with you."

Welcome back, happiness.

THE ALARM FROM his phone coming from the other side of the room woke him. He hated leaving the comfort of Belle's arms, but he had to be at work by seven. After last night, he couldn't afford to be late.

His bare feet hit the cold floorboards. He had to convince Belle to move into the main house sooner rather than later. He no longer saw any reason for her not to. It wasn't as though they weren't already married. Harlan watched Belle's sleeping form before he tore himself from the bed and turned off the alarm.

They deserved a proper honeymoon. That would be new to both of them. They hadn't had enough money for one when they planned their first wedding, and his shotgun marriage to Molly hadn't warranted one.

He stepped into his boxer briefs and tugged them on

as he gazed out the window overlooking their ranch. It was a long time coming, but it was finally theirs together. Maybe they'd even add to their little brood in the near future. It was more than wishful thinking. Last night had been the culmination of years of waiting to openly love Belle the way he should have eight years ago. He'd been wrong when he told Ivy they wouldn't have a happy-ever-after. Harlan wasn't a romantic man, but damned if Belle didn't bring it out in him.

A car idling at the entrance to his ranch caught his attention. The area around the vehicle was practically engulfed in exhaust. From what he could see, it didn't look familiar either. He had a vague recollection of Belle telling him someone was outside during the night. It had to be the same person. Not many people wandered onto his ranch.

He finished dressing and tugged on his boots. Lillie stood at the door of her carrier with a blanket half draped over her back. "Good morning, little one." He rubbed her head through the wire door. "Let me wake your mommy." A week and a half with Belle and he was already talking to the animals. "Belle, honey." He stroked the side of her cheek before placing a light kiss against it. "Lillie's waiting for you."

She slowly sat up in bed and blinked away the sleep. "Good morning." She smiled. He had waited far too long to wake up to that smile. "You're already dressed?"

"It's a little after six and I have to get to work. Did you try to tell me there was someone outside earlier?"

Belle nodded. "They were sitting at the entrance. I figured they made a wrong turn or something."

"Whoever it was is still there."

"What?" The sheet slipped down around her waist, exposing her breasts. It took every ounce of his strength not to spend the next hour or two making love to her again. "That's odd."

"I'll check it out." He gave her a quick kiss. "I'm sure it's nothing."

"Be careful." Belle watched him fasten his police duty belt before climbing out of bed. She wrapped the sheet around her and looked out the window. "That's the same spot they were in last night."

"I'll make us some coffee, too. And, Belle, I didn't realize how cold it was up here in the morning during the summer. You need to stay with your husband in the house. And we need to do a whole lot more of this." He pointed to the bed. "Much, much more."

Belle's cheeks flushed at his insistence. "Let's discuss it later. You have Ivy to consider."

"Fair enough." He tipped his hat. "I'll meet you up at the house."

The muscles in his legs ached as he descended the stable's stairs. The last time he'd had that intense of a workout was in the police academy. He gave the interior of the stables a quick scan before heading outside. As he approached the waiting car, the engine cut off and a woman stepped from it.

His heart stopped beating.

Molly.

MOLLY! EVEN FROM the second story of the stables Belle recognized her. Had she heard that Belle and Harlan had gotten married and rushed back to town to louse it up? "Brava, Molly." Belle clapped. "Your timing is impeccable."

She wanted to run downstairs and confront her former friend. And not just for her sake, but for Ivy's, too. It had been a long time coming, but she thought better of it. The last thing she needed to do was make a scene smelling like sex. Especially considering she lived in the stables and Harlan lived in the house. Molly would never let her live that down.

She trusted Harlan. Didn't she? She had to. Granted that hadn't worked in her favor where Molly was concerned in the past, but they had both grown since then. She couldn't fathom Harlan ever forgiving Molly for walking out on Ivy.

Belle took a deep breath and jumped in the shower. She did some of her best thinking in there. Maybe Molly would be gone by the time she dressed and went downstairs. Just in case, she took extra care applying her makeup, which she normally didn't put on before work. Horses and cattle didn't care what she looked like. Her grandmother always said women wore makeup to impress other women. She had never believed that statement until right now.

After feeding her animals, she casually strolled out the back of the stables with Lillie on a leash. The car was still out front, but Harlan and Molly were nowhere in sight. She wasn't sure what she had hoped to accomplish by sneaking around…maybe overhear a conversation? But there didn't seem to be anything or anyone to spy on.

"This is silly. I'm an adult and I just spent the night in my husband's arms. I am not scared of some has-been." Belle laughed to herself. "More like Molly never was."

She waited for Lillie to finish her business outside, and did a few chores in the barn before heading to the house for that long-overdue cup of coffee. It was almost seven. Both she and Harlan needed to leave soon. She still had to pick up her truck from the impound lot.

She entered the kitchen, not expecting to see Molly sitting at the table. Her first instinct was to claw the woman's eyes out. The second was to run and avoid the drama altogether. She had enough going on in her life and she didn't need whatever baggage Molly brought with her making it worse. Instead, she crossed the room to the coffeepot, feeling the burn of her ex-friend's stare against her back. Belle poured herself a cup and faced her.

"This is a surprise," Molly said without blinking.

You bet your sweet bippy it's a surprise. "I'm sure it is."

"How long have you two been together?" she asked.

"You mean how long have Belle and I been married?" Harlan corrected.

"Oh, well I guess you two finally got what you always wanted."

Belle scoffed. "You meant what you took from me."

"I never took Harlan from you." Molly remained impassive, still staring. "He had already left you when he and I got together. You're blaming the wrong person."

"I blame both of you." Belle closed the distance between them. "The two closest people to me stabbed me in the back. Romances come and go and if Harlan and I had broken up, that would have been one thing. But I thought of you as a sister. My grandmother treated you like a daughter. Your betrayal stunned me more than his. His hurt like hell, but yours broke every girl code out there." Belle held up her hands. "But I've moved past all of that."

"Clearly." Molly scanned her top to bottom. "I don't get it. Why did you two spend the night in the stables?"

"Because we have some orphaned animals and we're keeping a close eye on them," Harlan answered. "Not that it's any of your business."

"Molly, what do you want?"

"She wants Ivy," Harlan ground out. "And as I told her, over my dead body."

Chapter Eight

Belle was still reeling over Molly's arrival when she remembered this morning's court appearance. Once again, her life had done a complete one-eighty overnight.

She ran into the courtroom one minute before nine. Her court-appointed public defender waved to her from the front row. There was one good thing about remaining in the system…they always assigned her the same attorney. Jocelyn Winters. The two had become friends over the past few years and Belle held the woman solely responsible for keeping her out of jail.

Belle took her seat beside Jocelyn and scanned the room, wondering if Harlan had decided to come. That's if he even knew about today. She hoped he stayed far away. Well, as far away as the sheriff's department next door would take him. She'd already caused enough trouble for him.

"Oh, my God. What is she doing here?"

Jocelyn followed her gaze. "That's your stepdaughter, isn't it?"

"My what?" *Stepdaughter.* "Yes." Belle hadn't thought of herself as Ivy's stepmother. She guessed by law, she was. Her and Harlan's marriage was too new and fragile to place herself in a parental role. "She shouldn't be here."

Harlan had kept Ivy out of school today for fear Molly would try to contact her or even worse…take her. He needed the chance to notify everyone involved in her life before allowing her to go back to school or visit any of her friends. Belle had a suspicion all play-dates would be on Harlan's ranch for the foreseeable future. Ivy was supposed to be safely tucked away on the Silver Bells Ranch with Dylan. How on earth did she get into town?

Belle reached for her phone before she remembered they weren't allowed in court. Bryan sat in the front row behind the prosecutor. Belle stood to call his name when the judge entered the room.

"All rise for the Honorable Judge Beckett Sanders," the bailiff announced.

Crap!

"You may be seated," the judge commanded from the bench. "Who's first on today's docket?" he asked the bailiff.

"Belle Elizabeth Barnes."

The judge removed his glasses and rubbed his eyes.

"Step on up, Belle." Judge Sanders had ditched any formality when it came to her years ago. "I heard you got married. Congratulations."

"Yes, Your Honor." Belle couldn't resist smiling. Maybe court wouldn't be so bad. "I did. And thank you."

"Why are you standing before me today?"

"Honestly, I'm not sure which offense this is for,

Your Honor." Belle inwardly cursed herself. When had her life become so out of control she didn't know why she was in court?

The judge laughed and put his glasses back on. "That's not reassuring. Have you seen the inside of a jail cell this past month?"

"A few times, Your Honor." Belle braved a quick glance in Bryan's direction, hoping to get his attention.

"Will the prosecutor please read the charges against our resident rebel bride?"

"Miss Barnes is here for charges from July 4 and 11. Both are petty theft charges of property not exceeding $1,500 in value. Restitution has been paid to the property owners. If convicted, these two charges will put Miss Barnes over the third theft offense limit. In addition, there is one criminal trespass charge, which is associated with the petty theft on the eleventh."

"How do you plea?"

"Not guilty, Your Honor." Belle wanted to crawl into a hole and die. She wondered how many of the charges Ivy understood. Regardless, she was sure *theft* and *trespass* were two words she was familiar with.

"Do you wish to waive your right to a trial on another day or do you wish to proceed this morning?"

"Your Honor," Jocelyn began. "Miss Barnes would like to proceed today."

"Your Honor," Belle interrupted. "May I please approach the bench? It's urgent." He waved her forward and covered the microphone with his hand. "Judge Sanders, Harlan's daughter is in the back of the courtroom. I don't know how she got here, but she's supposed to be on the Silver Bells Ranch with Dylan.

Molly showed up this morning laying claim to Ivy, and Harlan fears she'll take her. Can Bryan bring her to her father? He may not even realize she's gone. But if he does, he'll be frantic."

"Deputy Bryan Jones, please approach the bench." Judge Sanders peered over his glasses.

Bryan was startled at the sound of his name. "Yes, Your Honor." He crossed the front of the courtroom.

"Miss Barnes needs to speak with you."

"Ivy's in the back of the courtroom alone," Belle whispered. "Do you know why she's here?"

"No." Bryan turned toward the little girl. "Where's Harlan?"

"I have no idea and with Molly running around I'm afraid something's wrong."

The judge leaned farther over the bench. "Deputy, how many cases do you have today?"

"Just one. Speeding ticket. Fifty-five in a twenty. I don't see the guy, though."

"Belle, are you certain you don't want to postpone your appearance?"

"What's the point? I was arrested on Tuesday for rescuing a piglet. I'll be here next month. I'd rather not have all my charges announced on one day. It's kind of humiliating."

"I'm sorry, it's what?" Judge Sanders stared at her. "I never thought I'd hear those words out of your mouth."

"I never thought my indiscretions, however honorable the reasons were, would be read in front of an impressionable seven-year-old girl."

The judge scrawled a few notes on the legal pad before redirecting his attention to them. "Deputy Jones, please take Ivy to her father and, Belle, you can return to the defendant's table."

Judge Sanders waited for Bryan and Ivy to leave the room before proceeding. "Will the prosecution please explain the nature of the charges?"

After a half hour of listening to the prosecutor read her priors, Belle wanted to throw up. Hadn't she paid attention in court before? None of it was foreign to her, yet she had a difficult time associating the person they were describing with herself. Being a rebel with a cause was one thing, but she sounded like a loose cannon. She was shocked Harlan even married her with this long of a record. He was right—her actions affected his career and Ivy's life.

If Judge Sanders convicted her on both petty theft charges today, he'd have no choice but to remand her to jail for the state-mandated thirty days. When he reduced her charges and gave her a hundred hours of community service and six months of probation instead, she felt luckier than a four-leaf clover. She made a solemn vow to herself never to see the inside of a courtroom again unless she was a witness for the prosecution. And there was that pesky last court appearance she needed to make on Lillie's behalf. But neither of those were third offenses. She'd never see the inside of a jail cell again.

How dare Molly storm back into their lives and demand to be a part of Ivy's life? He'd spent the better part of the morning calling in every favor owed to him from various law enforcement agencies around the country. He wanted a detailed report of her whereabouts and who she had been with since the day she left. People had asked if he kept tabs on her over the years and he never had. She hadn't been worth the time or effort involved. A judge had awarded him full custody and nothing else had mattered.

Sheriff Parker even made a few calls on his behalf. Molly was the definition of a *town pariah*. She hadn't a friend left in Saddle Ridge after walking out on their daughter the way she had. Speaking of his daughter, he wondered if she was still mad at him after he yelled at her this morning for taking off.

Dylan had an appointment and Harlan had to bring Ivy to work with him. After explaining his reason— Molly—the department understood. Unfortunately, Ivy hadn't. What kid wanted to go to school? His. And she was mad she was missing a science demonstration they'd been working on all week. How do you explain to your child you were protecting her from her own mother? He'd do everything in his power to prevent telling her Molly wanted to see her. Unless the court ordered it, he'd do his damnedest to keep it from happening. He refused to allow his daughter to ride the Molly Weaver roller coaster. It was a sickening ride fraught with hate and lies.

He realized hanging around the station bored her, but it was the safest place in town. Once Dylan came back, then she'd be safe on Silver Bells. But bored or not, sneaking out and into the courthouse next door because she saw Belle's truck pull into the adjoining lot had infuriated him. Truth be told, he was madder at himself for not realizing she was missing. Then he'd gone on the warpath and berated the courthouse security guard for letting her in without adult supervision. He may have gone a little overboard with his reaction, but today it had been warranted.

Ivy sat next to his desk sulking and coloring. She was confused and he didn't blame her for the attitude.

When lunchtime rolled around, he was no closer to understanding what had happened to Molly. Her record was clean. Dylan stopped by after his appointment to take Ivy back to his ranch. At least she'd have her puppy and the other animals to play with and keep her company.

He hadn't heard from Belle all morning, but he already knew she'd had a court appearance thanks to his daughter. Bryan said it hadn't gone well while he was there. Belle had been genuinely embarrassed that Ivy had heard her charges. In a way, he was glad that happened. Ivy hadn't asked him any questions, and maybe this was the kick in the rear Belle needed to straighten out her life. And considering she hadn't been paraded through the police station to a holding cell, he assumed the charges had been reduced. He wanted to spend the rest of his life with her and if last night was any indication of the future, they'd be very happy together.

Harlan had promised Belle he would stop by the nursing home and visit with Trudy at lunchtime. He should have gone sooner. It was a gorgeous day and Harlan opted to walk the few blocks. He waved hello to the nurses at the front desk as he turned down Trudy's hallway.

He froze outside her doorway, recognizing the woman's voice before he laid eyes on her.

"What the hell are you doing here?" Harlan glared at Molly, sitting beside Trudy's bed.

"I'm visiting—what does it look like?" Molly replied.

"Wasn't that nice of Molly to visit with me during her lunch hour?" Trudy patted Molly's arm. "I'll only be here for a few more days, then you can come visit me at the house."

"Molly, may I see you in the hallway please?" Harlan said between clenched teeth.

She shook her head. "What for?"

"Sit down, Harlan." Trudy pointed to the chair next to Molly.

"No, thank you, I'd rather stand. I've been sitting all day."

"Suit yourself." Trudy returned her attention to Molly. "Molly was just telling me why she wasn't at your wedding."

The careful facade Belle and he had built was beginning to crumble. "Yes, Molly. Why couldn't you attend our wedding? Come to think of it, we haven't seen you around in quite some time."

"Molly has a new job and it takes her out of town quite a bit."

"Is that so?" Harlan folded his arms across his chest. "Doing what?"

"Oh, my God! What are you doing here?" Belle stood in the doorway. She strode across the room and grabbed Molly by the back of the shirt, yanking her to her feet.

"Belle, what's wrong with you?" Trudy attempted to sit up straight.

"I'm sorry, Grammy. Molly has to cut her visit short. She's late for a doctor's appointment and she asked me to remind her. I'll show her out, but I'll be back in just a minute. Say goodbye, Molly."

"I'll see you again soon, Trudy."

Belle tugged her out into the hall, almost banging Molly's face against the door frame.

Harlan followed them. Half out of fear Belle would kill her and half for entertainment purposes.

Belle marched up to the security guard. "Do you see this woman? Take a good look at her. In fact, take her picture. She is never to come anywhere near my grandmother again. She is a menace and a threat to my family." Belle pushed open the front door of the nursing home and shoved Molly through it. "If I have to get a restraining order against you, I will. This is your one and only warning. My grandmother does not have the faculties to defend herself against you. You are not to come near her."

Harlan stepped in between them. "Molly, if you want to talk to me, then talk to me. But don't try to go through Trudy or try to get under Belle's skin to get my attention. I'm not above throwing you in jail."

"Oh, please do." Belle glared up at him.

"My intentions were only to visit with Trudy. I didn't mean to upset anyone." Molly turned to Belle. "I stopped by your grandmother's house only to discover you had sold it and she lived here. I had no idea."

"Why would you? You abandoned your family six years ago and never looked back. You wouldn't even recognize your own daughter if she was standing here."

"You're probably right. But I would love the opportunity." Molly handed Harlan a slip of paper. "I will give you some time to think it over. I'm staying here in town and if you don't allow me some form of visitation with my child, I will have the courts intervene."

"I don't know which is sadder," Harlan said. "The fact you think you can come back to town and pick up right where you left off, or that you think you have a chance of winning any form of custody or visitation with Ivy."

"This isn't the time or the place to discuss it." Belle looked over her shoulder. A small crowd had gathered in the nursing home's atrium.

"You're right," Molly agreed. "My number and my hotel are on that slip of paper. I would like to speak with you about Ivy, alone."

"Belle's my wife. She has every right to be a part of this conversation." The last thing Harlan wanted was to meet Molly in a hotel room alone. Not because he didn't trust himself. He had no interest in anyone other than his wife. He didn't trust Molly or how Molly might use this situation against Belle. He finally had everything he'd ever wanted with the woman of his dreams and he refused to allow anyone to come between them.

"Fine, just promise me we'll talk."

"We will talk. But it will be on my terms, in a location I choose, and if I suspect anything, there won't be any second chances. You're lucky I'm giving you this one."

"Understood." Molly began to walk away, then stopped and faced Belle. "I thought if anyone would understand, you would. Didn't I do what you always wanted your mother to do? I came back. How would you feel if you found out your mother had returned for you and nobody allowed you to see her? How would you feel knowing you could have had answers to all your questions, but someone stole that chance from you?"

"That's low, even for you, Molly," Harlan said.

"Please stay away from my grandmother." Belle headed inside.

"When we talk, you better be prepared to answer a lot of questions. Starting with where the hell have you been and how could you leave and never once contact our daughter? She doesn't even remember you. She hasn't the foggiest idea what you even look like and she's never asked. She doesn't give you a second thought." Molly winced at his comment as if he'd physically struck her. "What did you expect? You're not a part of her life. After you left, I wondered how this would affect her. I learned a child's resiliency is a beautiful thing. She bounced back like you never even happened. She didn't even cry, because the house was finally peaceful. When you were there, you weren't much of a mother. So wherever you went, I hope you found the help you needed. And if you ever have more children, and maybe you already do, I hope you have enough good sense and strength to treat them better than you treated Ivy."

Harlan strode into the nursing home and straight out the back door into the garden. He had finally said everything he'd wanted to say to Molly for six years. His body shook with relief. His shoulders released the tension he swore he'd been carrying all this time. It was over. The waiting and wondering if she would ever return. She had returned and he had to prepare for the fight of his life. Not that he thought he'd have much of one. Saddle Ridge was a small town in the middle of a small county. Everyone knew everyone else, and everyone knew what Molly had done. Outside of some fantastic medical excuse, nothing would make up for her abandonment.

"Harlan." Belle rested her hand on his shoulder. He covered it with his own, turned and gathered her in his arms, holding her tightly. His heart hammered in his chest as he buried his face in her hair. She wound her arms around his waist and stroked his back. "Molly's right," she said. "You should listen to what she has to say."

Chapter Nine

When Belle told Harlan he should give Molly a chance to explain, she didn't think he'd do it hours later. She was alone on the ranch for the first time at night since her arrival. It felt cold, lacking the charm and emotion without Harlan and Ivy. His daughter was still staying with Dylan and probably would for the next couple days.

Harlan had given her a key to the house and told her to make herself at home. And technically it was her home. Not just because they were married, but because she had been the one to persuade Harlan to buy the ranch years ago. She'd fallen in love with it the moment she stepped on the wide front porch. The whitewashed clapboard siding provided a neutral palette against the colorful western Montana backdrop. This had been where she planned to raise her kids. And as wonderful as last night had been, she doubted she'd get that chance. They'd already moved too fast. She'd initially excused it because of their past, but in the cold light of day, it was just plain foolishness. Neither one of them was ready for an emotional commitment. They'd slept together and now it was out of their system. It wouldn't happen again.

Lydia called with an update on the bull they rescued. Part of the front leg had to be amputated, but they knew of an animal prosthetic company willing to donate their time and materials to construct him a new limb. He had a long recovery ahead of him, but his quality of life had already improved dramatically.

After their conversation, Belle finished mucking the stalls, showered and ate dinner. She stared at the main house from the stable's apartment window. As much as she hated what Molly did to Harlan and Ivy, she'd pack up and leave in a heartbeat if it meant Ivy could have a happy home with both of her parents. Isn't that what every child deserved?

It was what she had always dreamed of. Not only had her mother abandoned her, she never knew who her father was. For that matter, her mother probably hadn't either. She'd always fantasized who Unknown could have been. Maybe somebody famous? Maybe a multimillionaire who would give her all the money she needed to start her rescue ranch. Whoever it was, she wished them well. Ivy at least had a name, she just hadn't had the opportunity to put a face to it yet. Now she would. And whatever happened between Molly, Harlan and their daughter was out of her hands. She wouldn't interfere.

The sound of Harlan's truck interrupted her thoughts. She held her breath, waiting to hear if he came in the stables or went to the main house. When the downstairs door didn't open, she braved a look out the window. The kitchen lights flicked on, followed by the upstairs bedroom a minute later. For a moment, Belle wondered if he was alone. Although, knowing Molly, she would've cackled from the truck to the back door to make sure Belle heard her.

She pulled her computer out of the tote bag next to her bed and turned it on. She prayed Harlan's Wi-Fi wasn't password protected because she needed to find a new apartment and fast. The sound of boots coming up the stable's stairs startled her. It couldn't be Harlan; he was already inside his house. She ran to the apartment door to lock it, just as it opened, knocking her to the floor.

"Oh, my God, Belle!" Harlan reached for her. "I am so sorry. What were you doing standing on the other side of the door?"

"Me?" Belle rubbed the side of her head. "I saw you turn the lights on inside your house and I thought you were a stranger coming up the stairs. Don't you knock?"

"I guess it hadn't dawned on me to knock before entering my own stables, but you're right. I should have given you that courtesy."

"Fair enough." She allowed Harlan to help her to her feet. "So, what happened? Unless you don't want to tell me?"

Harlan guided her to the bed. "Let me see your head. Are you sure you're okay?"

"It's just a bump. I'm hardheaded, in case you haven't already noticed." Levity, no matter how weak, seemed to be in order.

"I went into the house first because I figured that's

where you would be." He sat beside her. "I thought we settled that."

"And then you went to see Molly." Belle pulled away from him. The more he rubbed her head, the more it hurt. "I'm okay."

"What does seeing Molly have to do with you moving in with me?" He scooted back against the headboard.

"If you and Molly have a chance to work things out for Ivy's sake, I think you should take it." The words left an acrid taste in her mouth.

"Thank you, but I can make my own decisions." He lifted her hand and placed a light kiss in the center of her palm. "Getting back together with Molly is not an option." He smiled. It was a devastating smile. One that sent her stomach to the moon and back. "Thank you for persuading me to listen to what she had to say. I already knew most of it."

"Did she give you any details?" A part of her was curious what her former best friend had been up to since Belle's wedding day. The other part didn't care what happened to the woman. She chose the high road out of respect for Ivy.

"She admitted she hadn't been ready to raise a child back then. Pretty much the same way I wasn't ready to get married. Not that I'm trying to justify either situation." Harlan kicked off his boots and reached for Belle, urging her to sit between his legs. "She had always wanted to travel and get away from small-town life. And that's exactly what she did. She works as a travel agent out of Billings. She told me when we spent that one night together she wasn't trying to get pregnant."

He wrapped his arms in front of Belle, cocooning her against him. "At least that's something." She still had a hard time absorbing his admission that he and Molly had only had sex once. Ever. A part of her had been overjoyed; the other part had been furious he'd thrown away everything they had together for a roll in the hay.

"I think I needed to hear that, because I always wondered if she had purposely trapped me. I was partially to blame, but I don't think I was willing to admit it until recently."

"Does she want you back?" Belle squeezed her eyes shut and braced for the answer.

"No. And I wouldn't entertain the thought even if she did. She said she doesn't want to come between us. Belle, she seems genuinely happy that you and I found our way back to one another. She had assumed we had been married for years, not days. I didn't explain our situation because it's none of her business. Knowing her, she would turn our quickie marriage against me. She would like to speak with you and apologize."

Belle tensed. Molly and Harlan had a lot to work through. She and Molly did not. "Sounds like she's making amends as part of a twelve-step program."

"The same thought ran through my mind. But isn't the first step always admitting you have a problem? She never abused alcohol or drugs when we were together. She just wasn't emotionally ready to be a parent. Now she claims she is. She's twenty-seven, appears stable—at least on paper—and would like the chance to know her daughter."

"Will you allow Ivy to see her?"

He blew out a slow breath before answering. "I thought about what you said earlier…how you would have appreciated the same opportunity. I don't think I could live with myself if I didn't give Ivy the chance to decide on her own. She may not be ready to make that decision, and Molly will have to accept whatever the outcome. I won't force Ivy into this."

"Are you still worried about her running off with Ivy?" It had been her grandmother's biggest fear when Belle first came to Saddle Ridge. She remembered Trudy's stern warnings to never go with her mother under any circumstances. The situation hadn't presented itself and over time, the memories of her mother slowly faded.

"I'm more afraid if I take too long, she'll take it upon herself to meet Ivy, and that's what I want to avoid. My daughter is already confused. I don't think I can keep it from her any longer. It's too late tonight. I'll talk to her first thing tomorrow morning. I think this will be the hardest conversation of my life. In the meantime, will you please move into the house with us?"

Belle shook her head. "I can't."

"Why?" Harlan swept the hair off her shoulder and shifted his body to see her expression.

She withdrew from his arms and turned around to face him. "Your daughter will experience the biggest shock of her young life tomorrow. I don't think now is the time to introduce another change into her safe zone." She reached for his hands and held them between her own. "Your house and everything it represents is home. She has you and Elvis and that's all she needs right now." Harlan opened his mouth to protest, but she pressed a finger to his lips to silence his words. "I'm added confusion. I don't want Ivy to feel she must choose between me or her mother. You have some big adjustments coming on the horizon. Take this time for you and your daughter."

"What are you saying?" The pain was evident in his eyes. "Are we breaking up?"

"We're married." She smiled, however bittersweet. "We can't break up without a divorce." Belle attempted to laugh, but her heart ached too much and it terrified her. "I think it's best if I stay out here. We're moving way too fast. That doesn't mean we can't still spend time together, because I do want that." She ran the backs of her fingers down the side of his face and cupped his chin. "I want us to both be sure we're making the right decision."

Harlan gently eased her down onto the bed, his touch light as he skimmed his fingertips over her hips through the thin cotton fabric of her boxer shorts. "I've already made my decision. I made it the day I married you." His lips grazed hers. "I may have screwed up our relationship the first time, but I would never break my wedding vows."

His hand moved under her shirt, searing a path across her abdomen. A shiver of arousal shot through her. A tiny moan caught in her throat as he lifted her shirt and his lips found her bare breasts.

"No, no, no." Belle scooted out from under him. "Sex clouds things."

Harlan sat on the edge of the bed, slack jawed. "Please tell me you're kidding."

Belle groaned. "I'm not." Saying no to a night of

passion was proving harder than she thought. Especially when every inch of her body yearned for him. But it twisted her emotions. Despite what he said about Molly, she wasn't ready to chance him walking out a second time. Wisdom comes from experience, and she wouldn't make the same mistake twice.

THE FOLLOWING MORNING, Harlan paced the length of his living room. Dylan was due to arrive with Ivy any minute and he still hadn't figured out how to tell his daughter her mother wanted to meet her.

To make matters worse, he was still nursing his wounds from Belle's rejection last night. As much as he hated to admit it, she was right. They were moving too fast and her moving in would probably be too much for Ivy to handle on top of Molly. It gave him one more reason not to like his ex-wife.

No sooner had Dylan pulled up outside than Harlan heard his daughter's laughter permeate the air. "Daddy, I'm home." She barreled through the screen door, Elvis clutched tight to her chest.

He lowered himself onto the kitchen chair, wrapping his arms around her and her little charge. "And how are you two this morning?"

"We're good. Elvis is learning to do potty outside."

"Only after Elvis did many potties inside." His eldest brother, Dylan, stood in the doorway.

"I didn't even think about that when I sent him over there with her." Harlan cringed. "Did he ruin any of your hardwood floors? Whatever damage he did, let me know so I can pay for it."

"Nah. We had it covered."

"Yeah, Daddy." Ivy beamed up at him. "We had it covered with lots of newspapers all over the house."

Dylan nodded behind her. "Will you two be okay? Do you need anything?"

"I think we're good. And thank you again for watching her."

"Anytime, little brother. Ivy's a treat any day." Dylan slapped him on the shoulder. "Call me later."

"Is Belle here?" Ivy placed Elvis on the floor and ran into the living room, the puppy hot on her heels.

"No, honey. She's not." Harlan followed her into the living room and joined her on the large area rug. "She had to go to work."

"How come you're not at work and why won't you let me go to school?"

"Because today's Saturday and you and I both have the day off." Harlan swallowed down the bile threatening to creep up his throat. "Daddy needs to talk to you about something. Or rather someone."

"Who?" She slowly stroked Elvis's back. The puppy's eyes were heavy with sleep. They had probably played nonstop ever since he dropped them off at Dylan's on Thursday night.

"Your mommy." There, he said it. He hadn't had to share Ivy with anyone for six years and the thought of doing so now terrified him. Ivy had only ever spent time with his family, and in recent years, that had been narrowed down to Dylan and his uncle Jax. "Would you like to meet your mommy?"

Ivy shrugged and curled up on the floor, wrapping her arms around Elvis. Harlan brushed the hair out of her face.

"Are you tired or don't you want to talk about Mommy?"

"I don't know." Fear laced her tiny voice.

"I'm not asking you to go live with your mommy." This wasn't fair. A child shouldn't be afraid of their parents. Yet the thought of meeting her mother reduced his daughter to a shell of who she'd been minutes earlier. He hated Molly for instilling that fear. "I just wondered if you wanted to spend some time with her. It could be for however long or short you want it to be. If you only want to see her for a minute, you can. If you want to spend an hour with her, you can do that, too. I will be there with you the entire time so you won't have to worry about being left alone with her."

"I want Belle to be my mommy."

While the idea alone made him smile, he didn't want Ivy to get her hopes up. Which was exactly why Belle hadn't wanted to move into the house. She understood his daughter's needs more than he did, and that didn't sit well with him. He'd allowed their relationship to distract him from what was most important. Ivy. "That's not going to happen right now."

"Is Mommy going to move in with us?" She traced the pattern of the area rug with her index finger, and Harlan wondered what other thoughts were running through her head.

"Absolutely not." It didn't matter how wonderful of a bond Ivy may form with Molly in the future; the woman would never live in his house again. "Our house is for you, me and Elvis. This house is yours as much as it is mine. We've always made decisions together and we will continue to do that."

"Where has Mommy been?"

And there was the question he'd dreaded the most. He didn't have an answer. Molly didn't have one either. Except she needed time to grow up.

"Sometimes when people have babies, they are not emotionally ready to take care of them. Do you understand what I mean by *emotionally*?"

Ivy shook her head.

"Let's use Elvis as an example. Say we got him when you were in preschool instead of second grade. Do you remember preschool?"

Ivy nodded. Harlan guessed a nod was better than no response at all.

"Can you imagine if you'd had Elvis then? You weren't a big girl like you are now. Elvis would have been sad because you would have forgotten about him and wouldn't have known how to care for him. That's kind of what happened with your mommy. She wasn't ready to take care of you, but instead of ignoring you and making you feel bad every day, she left until she felt she was ready to give you the attention you deserve. Just like you give Elvis the attention he deserves. Does that make any sense?"

Harlan rolled his eyes at his own analogy, praying she made the connection.

"Mommy's a big girl now?"

"I certainly hope so," Harlan muttered.

"Do I have to see her?"

"You don't have to do anything you don't want to do. Ever. Except for going to school and doing your homework."

"But you won't let me." Her big blue eyes were

glassy with tears. Hurting his daughter had been the last thing he wanted.

"On Monday you will go back to school and everything will be normal again."

"I don't understand why I couldn't before."

"Because your daddy had to take care of some things with Mommy and while he did that I needed you to stay with Dylan. Now that everything is settled, you can go back to school."

He hated lying to his daughter. Visitation was far from settled. But he had to swallow his own fears and allow his daughter to live a normal, healthy life until he could straighten things out with Molly.

"Can I sleep on it?" Ivy asked.

Harlan covered his mouth to keep from laughing out loud. Every time Ivy had asked him if they could get a dog, he told her he had to sleep on it. At least she was paying attention.

"You can take all the time you need." Harlan lay down beside her and pulled her close to him. "Daddy's in no rush."

"WE HAVE PLENTY of room for you to stay here if it's getting too uncomfortable on the ranch," Lydia said as she examined Lillie's sunburn on Saturday afternoon.

"Thank you, I appreciate it. I wish I had a place on the other side of the ranch already. It would make life a lot easier. Then there'd be some distance without there being too much of one. If that makes any sense." It was awkward and uncomfortable living so close to Harlan, knowing Molly was trying to reestablish a relationship with her daughter. It would have been different if she'd helped raise Ivy for the last six years. "Molly and I are both new to her. I don't want to confuse her, but I'm not sure I'm entirely ready to walk away either. I should have never moved in there."

"Your fears about Harlan and Molly reconnecting and Ivy's best interest aside, how are you doing?"

Her heart was equally as strong as it was fragile. Her mind ran in overdrive until it made her dizzy, and the butterflies in her belly hadn't stopped fluttering since the day she and Harlan had exchanged vows.

"It's ironic. Yesterday morning, I sat in the courtroom horrified by my own police record. It's like I finally got it. I won't stop doing what I do, but I understand more of what you and Harlan have been trying to tell me. I wanted to share that revelation with Harlan and see if I could truly forgive him. Until I completely do that, we don't have a chance. And then Molly entered the picture. It's hard to forgive and forget with that reminder staring me in the face."

"You can't—not even for a single second—believe Harlan stopped loving you because Molly sashayed into town?"

"Who said anything about love?"

"It's written all over both of your faces. Calvin and I saw it in the dark in the middle of a cattle ranch. It's obvious. Keep telling yourself otherwise and you're the only one you're lying to."

"Our timing is off." Belle scratched under Lillie's chin. She was surprised the piglet had allowed Lydia to examine her this long without a single protest. "He has his hands full with Ivy and I have mine full with Trudy. I need to spend more time at the nursing home. I haven't been there as much this past week. She won't be around for much longer, at least not in a lucid capacity. I love being with Harlan and Ivy, but it's taking away from the time I normally spend with my grandmother."

"Your grandmother would want you to have fun and enjoy yourself." She handed Lillie to Belle. "Her back looks better. Your grandmother's the one who wanted you to marry Harlan. You did this for her."

"Only because she didn't know better."

"Because I love you dearly, I'm calling bull on that." Lydia tugged off her examination gloves and tossed them in the trash bin. "You were looking for a good enough excuse to talk to Harlan and don't you tell me otherwise. I've spent enough time around you to notice when you're pining for a man. We are in contact with some of the hottest single cowboys in the state and no matter how many times you've been asked out, you either go on one date or you turn them down altogether. You compare them all to Harlan whether you realize it or not."

Belle hated that there was some truth to that statement. She'd spent the last eight years comparing every man she met to the man who broke her heart. She thought it was to protect herself from getting hurt again. Now she realized it was the opposite. No man could permeate the shield she'd built around her heart, except Harlan. Only he held the key. The problem was, she'd changed the locks long ago.

Chapter Ten

"Please don't go." Harlan stood in the middle of the stable the next morning. "My daughter and I need you here. Not at Lydia's." Belle had already begun packing what little there was of her belongings and planned to move what she could into her friend's spare bedroom tomorrow morning. "You won't have any privacy over there. If you want to stay in the apartment above the stables, that's fine. I'll get a couple of space heaters to warm up the place. But you can't leave. Besides, Ivy's in love with Imogene and it would break her heart if she left."

Belle gave the man credit. He knew how to play the kid card to perfection. "Ivy can have Imogene. I think she'd be very happy staying here on your ranch, as long as you keep her safe."

"We will, thank you." Harlan removed his hat and took a step toward her. "And what about you? Wouldn't you be happy staying here on the ranch? I promise to keep you safe."

The man made her knees weak with a simple turn of phrase. She tilted her head back and groaned. He closed the remaining space between them and kissed the tender spot at the base of her throat.

"That's not playing fair." Belle allowed him to trail a few more kisses along her collarbone before she broke from his grasp. "Don't you want time alone with your daughter to sort the Molly situation out? I'm always around when Ivy's home. Either she's out in the stables with me or we're all in the house together."

"I won't lie. I've thought about that, too, but you bring out a joy and happiness in Ivy I haven't seen before."

"That's only because I gave her a puppy."

"Don't belittle that connection, Belle. Please." Harlan took her hands in his. "You've had a very positive effect on her and I'd like it to continue, regardless of where you and I stand. You'll be here once the rescue center opens and I feel more comfortable with her getting to know you with me around. It shows her I'm okay with your relationship. She doesn't have another woman to confide in or talk to about female things. The woman who watches her after school is great, but she's not the warm and fuzzy type like you."

Belle laughed and returned to spreading fresh hay around Samson's stall. She'd never heard herself described as warm and fuzzy before. She kind of liked it. But the fact remained—Molly had returned and that was the bond he needed to foster.

"She has her mother now."

"Ivy hasn't agreed to meet Molly yet and I'm not forcing the issue either. Even if that all goes well, she won't be around 24/7. That's a definite. But you will be. Here or the other side of the ranch, you'll be on the property."

"Okay, okay." Belle stepped into the corridor and closed the stall door. "I'll stay."

"Great." Harlan's arm slid around her waist as he whirled her against his chest. His mouth claimed hers the way no other man could as his fingers splayed in her hair, drawing her even closer as he deepened their kiss. "I'll change your mind about me, however long it takes." His breath was warm against her lips. "Now I need you to do me a favor," he murmured.

"Yes." Belle barely recognized the sound of her own voice.

Harlan pulled away abruptly. "Will you watch Ivy? We're out of milk and I need to run to the store. She's in the house watching cartoons. I'm sure she'd love it if you joined her."

"Oh, I get it now." She playfully swatted him. "You just want a free babysitter."

"Be careful, you're assaulting a police officer. Don't make me handcuff you." He ran to his cruiser and hopped in before she attacked him again. He cracked the window an inch. "Bye, honey. I'll be back in a few."

She watched him drive away before heading into the house. "How are you doing, kiddo?" Belle plopped beside Ivy and Elvis on the couch while *Phineas and Ferb* played on the wide screen. She didn't watch much television but she recognized the cartoon as one of Lydia's boys' favorites. She didn't even own a TV, probably because her grandmother had never been big on it. Except for *Wheel of Fortune*. Trudy loved that show.

"I'm okay. I have a mommy now." Ivy's voice was just barely audible.

Belle reached for the remote and turned down the sound. "Do you want to talk about it?"

Ivy shifted Elvis onto her lap and wrapped her arms around him. "Does that mean you have to go away?"

"Only if you and your daddy want me to." Belle hated the sadness etched across the little girl's face.

Ivy shook her head. "Daddy says she wants to see me. What if she still doesn't like me?"

Belle swallowed hard, trying her best not to cry. "Honey, she didn't leave because she didn't like you. She left because she was confused." *Among other things.* "Maybe she has something good to tell you. She came a long way to see you, so that counts for something, right?"

Belle couldn't believe she was defending Molly in any capacity. It was none of her business and Harlan would probably kill her, but Belle had firsthand experience of what it was like to be the abandoned kid. Many of her fears and questions would probably be answered in one meeting.

"Maybe. I'll sleep on it some more." Ivy returned her attention to the television, effectively ending their conversation.

A few minutes later, Belle's phone rang. The number was unfamiliar but she answered it anyway. "Hello."

"It's Molly—please don't hang up."

You've got to be kidding me. The sound of Molly's voice reverberating in her ear made her ill. Belle's left eye started to twitch. "How did you get my number?"

She stood from the couch and walked out onto the porch.

"I took a chance you still had the same one." Her voice didn't sound as confident over the phone as it had in person.

Lucky me.

"I wondered if we could meet later and talk."

"I have plans today." *Not really.* "And my schedule is pretty tight during the week between work and my grandmother. In case I wasn't clear before, allow me to reiterate. I don't want you anywhere near the nursing home. You and Harlan may have come to some sort of an understanding, but that doesn't change anything between you and me."

"Would you be able to meet me for breakfast before work tomorrow?"

Belle rolled her shoulders. "We are not sitting down to a meal together. There might be a slim chance of that happening in the future, but not tomorrow or even next month."

"Okay, I get it. I won't bother you again."

Crap! Belle hated the sound of dejection. Either Molly was really good or Belle was really weak. "Coffee. We can meet for one cup of coffee. To go. We'll walk to the park and back."

"Thank you. Seven o'clock?"

"Six. I work on ranches all day. We get up before the roosters."

"Six it is. I noticed that little coffee shop is still in town. Meet there?"

"Sure. See you tomorrow."

Belle disconnected the call and sat on the porch

steps. She drew her knees to her chest and waited for Harlan's return. Ivy's laughter carried through the screen door. As long as she was laughing Belle didn't need to go inside and babysit. Her nerves were too on edge and she was afraid Ivy would pick up on her tension.

Harlan drove up a few minutes later and joined her on the top step. "Are you all right?"

"I just finished making a coffee date with your ex."

"No, you didn't." Harlan smiled.

She exhaled deeply, and all humor drained from his face. "You did?"

"She wanted to meet today, but I told her no. I need to spend some time at the nursing home. Then she asked if I would meet her for breakfast tomorrow. I compromised with coffee."

"Should I send a deputy over for police protection?"

"Molly may be many things, but she's not physically aggressive. I'll be okay."

"I meant to protect her." Harlan jumped up and ran in the house.

"Oh, very funny!" she called after him, relishing the sound of his laughter. Ivy and Harlan had similar laughs. His was deeper, of course, but they both threw their heads back when they found something humorous and laughed with their entire bodies.

He brought her out a mug of coffee a few minutes later. "Penny for your thoughts?"

"Thank you." She sipped the hot brew. "I'm just taking it all in. I never noticed some of the peaks in the mountains." The sun had been up for a couple of hours and cast highlights and shadows over the Swan

Range. "We grew up with them always being the back-drop of our daily lives, and their beauty was the major reason why I chose this house, but I don't think I've ever sat and looked at them. The last time I hiked them was probably junior high. I remember the views of the Swan Valley and Saddle Ridge were breathtaking, but I haven't done it again. I'm always going. Never stopping to appreciate what's around me."

"Wow. You're right. Ivy's seven and I haven't taken her on any hikes or trail rides. Dylan has her on the back of a horse all the time and occasionally she'll ask to ride here in the corrals. I ride this ranch all the time. She's never with me, though. We need to change that." He stood and held out his hand to her. "What are you doing today?"

"I plan to spend the afternoon with my grand-mother." She reveled in the feel of his palm against hers. "I'm free the rest of the day."

Harlan released her and leaned into the kitchen. "Ivy, go put on your riding clothes. We're taking the horses out into the valley this morning."

The sound of her bare feet smacking the floorboards as she ran up the stairs echoed all the way outside.

"No arguments from her, are there?" Belle laughed. "You mentioned earlier that she hadn't agreed to meet Molly. What happened?"

"Well, we had our talk. She didn't react with any enthusiasm. In fact, she didn't react to much at all. I asked her if she wanted to see her mother and she told me she had to sleep on it."

Belle knew she shouldn't laugh, but she couldn't

help herself. "That's too funny. I wonder where she got that from?"

"She's a regular chip off the old block."

"I remember when your dad used to say that."

Growing up, most of her friends had two parents and had been unable to relate to her only having a grandmother for family. As she got older, more people in her life lost their parents to death or divorce. She'd always felt a disconnect when she was around Harlan's massive family, despite their enormous generosity toward her. Now Harlan and Ivy both experienced that loss and emptiness. She'd never had it to miss. It must be much worse for them.

"Do you want me to saddle the horses?" she asked, not wanting to interrupt his thoughts.

"I'm right behind you." He tugged his hat down lower. "We'll take Outlaw, Dillinger and Clyde."

Belle smiled at his choice of names. She'd seen them etched on wooden plaques in front of the stalls, but hadn't had a chance to acknowledge them before. "I'm sensing a definite theme with you."

"I love my outlaws," he whispered in her ear as he strode past her.

Her mile-wide smile betrayed any composure she fought to control. *Did he just tell me he loved me?* He stopped at the tack room entrance and held the door for her, winking as she passed under his arm. *Oh, my God! I think he just did.*

THE BACK OF a horse was Harlan's second home. He'd wanted to be one of two things when he was growing up: the sheriff or a horse trainer. He still had a while to go before he made sheriff, but he had trained every one of the five horses in his stables.

Ivy rode between the two of them along the Swan River. His neighbor's ranch bordered the water and he had told Harlan he could ride their trails anytime. He'd had all this magnificent beauty at his fingertips and his daughter had been inside watching television every weekend. From this day forward, he vowed to plan something outdoorsy for them to do as a family at least one day a week.

"Daddy, is that snow?" Ivy pointed halfway up one of the mountains.

Harlan smiled. "No, baby, that's not snow. Snow doesn't move."

Belle reined her horse to a stop and followed their gaze. "They're mountain goats. That's a whole bunch of them for us to be able to see them like this."

"Remember our class trip to Glacier National Park?" Harlan asked.

"When the mountain goats were running alongside our red Jammer buses on Going-to-the-Sun Road? I kept thinking they'd run in front of us, but they didn't."

"That's the only bus we were allowed to stand up in and not get yelled at."

"You're not allowed to stand in the bus, Daddy. It's against the rules."

"You can in these, sweetie. They're vintage buses from the 1930s with a roll-back top, kind of like Uncle Jax's convertible. When you stop at various points throughout the park, you can stand up and take photos out of the roof." Harlan shook his head and looked at Belle. "Why am I explaining this to her when I can make reservations and take her there? We're only a little over an hour away."

"She's never been to Glacier National Park? It's practically in your backyard."

Harlan didn't have a response. He was ashamed to admit the idea never entered his mind. Here he had prided himself on being such an amazing single dad, at least by his standards, and he'd neglected to do anything meaningful with his daughter. Instead, he had relied on his older brother to do it for him.

"There are going to be quite a few changes around here."

Belle nudged Dillinger toward him. "I didn't mean to imply you were a bad father."

"You didn't." Harlan reached for her hand. "I'm glad you said something, though. I've missed out on too much of her life and she's been right in front of me the entire time."

They spent the rest of the morning exploring along the river before heading home for lunch. A million ideas ran through his head. Belle probably wouldn't be able to join them for some of their outings because of her schedule, but they'd make it work. Molly kept creeping into his thoughts. If she insisted on forcing the visitation issue, she'd probably have to come along on some of their trips. She lived almost seven hours away in Billings, but had told Harlan she'd consider relocating if things went well with Ivy. Selfishly he hoped they wouldn't. For Ivy's sake, he prayed they would. As much as he despised what Molly had done to them, he didn't want his daughter to grow up wondering what if. He'd already watched one child live through that nightmare, and Belle was only beginning to come into her own.

"I SHOULD HEAD OUT." Belle finished loading his dishwasher with their lunch plates then dried her hands. "I'm not sure when I'll be back tonight. I may stay for the dinner service." She gave Ivy a kiss on the forehead before they stepped onto the porch. "Thank you for a wonderful morning."

Harlan slid his fingers into the belt loops of her jeans and tugged her to him. "Have I convinced you to stay permanently yet?" He widened his stance so he could look into her eyes. "You've always been a part of this ranch, you just haven't realized it."

"You're not playing fair again." She'd had another taste of family life today and it excited her down to her toes. It's what she had always wanted. "I need to get to the nursing home." She leaned in as her lips grazed his, softly at first as the anticipation thickened the air in her lungs. Her fingers brushed the nape of his neck and she felt the hair rise at her touch. Her mouth moved over his, unapologetically firm as her tongue sought his. It was the first kiss she'd initiated since they'd married. And she liked it. Maybe a real relationship with Harlan wouldn't be so bad. "I'll see you later."

"Talk about not fair," Harlan called after her.

Belle practically skipped to the stables. She fed and checked on the animals before heading into town. She uncovered a new sense of wonderment when it came to Harlan. She'd always been drawn to the man, and even fascinated by him from afar. Unbeknownst to him, or anyone else for that matter, she'd been there the day he graduated from the police academy. She'd worn a brunette wig and borrowed a dress of her grandmother's so no one would recognize her. And the day he'd been promoted to deputy sheriff, she'd watched the courthouse steps ceremony from the window of the stationery store across the street. The need to be a part of the monumental moments in his life had always confounded her. She'd have sworn on her life to anyone who'd listen that she'd gotten over him the day he left her in the church. But she'd lied to everyone, including herself.

The nursing home parking lot was full, forcing her to park next door. Sundays were their busiest days. It looked like it was someone's birthday judging by all the balloons when she walked in. She solemnly wondered if her grandmother's birthday in November would be her last.

Think happy thoughts. It was sometimes hard to do in a nursing home.

"Hi, Grammy." Belle stepped into the room and gave her grandmother a kiss on the cheek. "You look good today."

"Thank you, dearie." Trudy's eyes seemed to stare right past her. "Have you seen my granddaughter out there?"

"Y-your granddaughter?" Belle's throat squeezed shut as her heart ceased beating for a second or two. "What's her name?"

"Belle." Her grandmother attempted to lean forward and get a better view of the hallway. "I hear noise out there. Could you check for me? She has blond hair and blue eyes, much like yours, only she's ten years old."

Belle nodded, unable to speak. She pointed to the doorway indicating she'd go check. Out in the hallway, she covered her mouth with both hands and slid down the wall to the floor. It was too soon. It was much too soon. She couldn't lose her yet. *Please, Lord, not yet.*

Myra joined her on the floor and handed her a pack of tissues. "Dry your eyes, honey." She wrapped an arm around Belle's shoulder and gave it a firm squeeze. "She's been in and out all morning. We think it's because of all the commotion going on today. Three residents are celebrating birthdays and there have been a lot of kids running up and down the hallway." Myra stood and lifted Belle by the arm. "Let's get you up before someone or something runs you over. I know you're opposed to us moving her to the Alzheimer's wing and we won't until you give us the authorization, but it's much quieter in that section. The environment is more stable and that has a big impact on their demeanor."

"She hates the quiet." Belle wiped her eyes. "She always had the classic country channel on the radio playing at home. I feel like I'm stuffing her away in a closet if I move her there."

"You're not," Myra reassured. "You're providing her with the best possible care you can. And we can play the radio for her. We can start that today."

"I don't know why I hadn't thought of the music before." Belle wiped her eyes.

"Because this is a stressful situation," Myra said.

"I'm okay now. Thank you."

"Give what I said some thought and feel free to ask us any questions you might have. We're here for you."

Belle nodded in acknowledgment and walked back into the room. "I couldn't find her out there."

"Find who?" Trudy asked. "Belle, bubbe. Why do you look like you've been crying?"

Belle started to laugh out of relief. "It's just allergies, Grammy. Now that I'm living on the ranch with Harlan, I'm around a lot more hay."

"That Harlan is a good man. Don't let him slip away."

"I won't, Grammy." Belle pulled a chair alongside the bed. "What have you been up to today? Have you gotten out of your room?"

A toddler duck-waddled down the hallway with his mother close behind him. "Slow down, Trevor."

"Oh, sure. I was in the garden waiting for my granddaughter earlier, but she never showed."

She sighed. "I'm sure she'll be here soon." Belle hoped the visitors thinned out sooner rather than later. There was so much she wanted to tell her about Harlan and the ranch. She'd have to skip the Ivy parts, but she had already thought of a little white lie she could tell to explain her presence in their lives. "Why don't you tell me about her." Belle played along while she waited for her grandmother to come back around.

"My little bubbeleh. Wild as she is sweet. She gets that from her mother. The wild, not the sweet. I don't know where we went wrong with Cindy. She'd always been a shy little thing until she grew the boobies."

Belle sucked in her lips to keep from laughing. She'd never heard her grandmother talk much about her mother before. While the memory of her mom's face had blurred over time, she did remember how *blessed* Cindy had been in the cleavage department.

"Those boobies got her in more trouble. Especially when she started dating that man who had been far too old for her. What twenty-seven-year-old goes out with a high school senior? When her father and I found out she told him she was eighteen, we put a stop to it. By that point it was too late."

Wait a minute. Belle perched on the edge of her chair. "What do you mean it was too late?"

"Cindy got herself pregnant with that man's baby. Her father got so upset he had a heart attack and died that very night."

Belle was afraid to breathe. She'd never known that's when her grandfather had died. The heart attack hadn't been a secret, but the circumstances surrounding it must have been. And all these years she'd been told her mother had been young and reckless and didn't know who Belle's father was. Her mind raced in a million directions. *Okay, deep breath.* She needed to sort fact from fiction. Trudy had Alzheimer's disease so she may not even be talking about her mother. There might be a different Cindy. Maybe she mixed up the names. *Names. She needed more names.*

"What happened to the man when Cindy got pregnant?"

"Turns out he wasn't so bad after all. Probably would have done her a world of good if she'd married him. He became a successful attorney and now Beckett's a judge."

The room began to suffocate her. She needed to get air. Desperately. *Judge Sanders?* How many judges were named Beckett? She stood, grabbing on to the bed rail for support. "I'll be right out—" The room tilted as darkness washed over her. The last thing she remembered before she hit the floor was her grandmother yelling for help.

Chapter Eleven

"Belle." Harlan patted her hand. "Belle, it's Harlan. Can you hear me?"

Her eyes felt heavy and her head ached something awful. She lifted her free hand, but something was attached to her fingertip. "What the heck?" She tried to shake the plastic contraption off when she noticed the wires coming out of her hospital gown. *Hospital gown?* "Where am I?"

"You're in the hospital. You fainted at the nursing home and they couldn't wake you up. Trudy said your head bounced off that floor like a basketball."

"I passed out?" Belle squeezed her eyes shut and tried to remember what had happened. Her grandmother hadn't recognized her. No, that wasn't it. She had recognized her after a while.

A nurse came in and interrupted her thoughts. "You're awake. How are you feeling?"

"My head hurts." Her tongue stuck to the roof of her mouth. "May I have some water?"

"I'll get it." Harlan poured her a cup from a mauve pitcher while the nurse checked the machines she seemingly had been connected to during her unconsciousness. Belle looked up at the IV bag hanging from the stand next to the bed and followed the drip line into her arm. She frantically grabbed at it. "What is this?" A wave of nausea slammed into her and dragged her under. "I feel sick."

"Shh." Harlan stuck a straw in the cup and handed it to her. "They're just fluids. You're dehydrated and you have a concussion."

"The doctor will be in to check on you shortly," the nurse said before walking out of the room.

"You gave me quite a scare." Harlan raked his hand through his thick chestnut hair. "Do you remember anything?"

Belle sipped her water. Flashes of memories from throughout the day churned in her brain. "I remember Grammy telling me my grandfather had a heart attack and died the night my mom told them she was pregnant."

"Whoa. That's heavy." He squeezed her hand. "Myra told me Trudy didn't recognize you today."

Belle tried to shake her head, but the pain was too intense. "She didn't. I guess the noise in there was too much for her to process. She thought I was ten and kept looking for me. She realized who I was for a little while, but then it was gone. Myra said that sometimes happened in loud situations."

"Do you remember feeling sick?"

"No." Belle closed her eyes against the brightness of the room. "We were talking about my mom. And boobies. I remember boobies."

Harlan bowed his head as his shoulders bounced up and down.

"Stop laughing at me." Belle tried to swat him but ended up clunking him in the head with her finger pulse oximeter. "Oh, I'm sorry."

"Are you trying to injure me so I'll join you in that bed?"

"Oh, my God!" Belle tried to sit up. Her mind almost short-circuited. Bed. Sex. Babies. Beckett. Sanders. "Judge Sanders is my father."

"What?" Harlan jumped up. "Are you serious?"

"And how's our patient this afternoon?" The doctor entered the room. "I'm Dr. Kim, the neurologist on staff. Are you experiencing any nausea?"

"I almost threw up a minute ago." Belle didn't take her eyes of Harlan. "My head really hurts."

The doctor withdrew a flashlight from his pocket and shined it in her eyes. "Will you follow the light for me?"

The light was bright, too bright. "When can I go home?"

"Not until at least tomorrow. Your pupils are even, so that's a good sign. Are you experiencing any blurry vision?"

"No."

"Your scan results were normal. We'll reevaluate you in a couple hours. Depending on how you feel, we may run another scan. You took quite a fall and you have a good-size knot on the side of your head. Your nausea concerns me, so we're going to keep you here overnight. I'll be back to check on you later. If you feel any worse than you do now, let us know right away."

"Thank you." He left the room and Harlan returned to her side.

"Are you sure she said Judge Sanders?"

"Granted my memory's a little fuzzy right now, but she said the man was ten years older than my mom and he thought she was eighteen. Then something about my grandparents telling him the truth. I guess she was already pregnant when the relationship ended. Grammy said she shouldn't have come between them because Beckett went on to become a judge." She shrugged. "Who else could it be?"

"Okay. But you were born in Texas."

"My mom was a runaway. I don't know if she left or if Grammy threw her out after my grandfather's heart attack. She blames my mom for his death. I never knew how or why she was in Texas. I assumed she ran away first and got pregnant down there. Apparently not. It makes sense, when you think about it. All the crap I've been arrested for, and I've always got off easy."

"Yeah, you have," Harlan agreed. "I've always said you had a guardian angel. I guess you just had a guardian."

"I need you to find him and get him to come see me." Belle reached for Harlan. "Tonight."

"Don't you want to wait until we get you home? I don't know anything about his personal life or where he lives."

"If you plan to be sheriff one day, you can figure out his address or phone number. I've waited twenty-seven years to meet my father. Soon he'll be my only living relative. I have questions. Lots of them, and they can't wait." She glanced around the room. "Where's Ivy?"

"With Dylan."

"I want her to spend the night with you, not him. I

won't let you spend the night here, worrying about me, when that child needs you now more than ever. I'm in good hands. So please, find Judge Sanders. Tell him it's urgent but don't tell him the truth. Let him think I'm in trouble again. I'm willing to bet he'll come to my rescue."

"Are you sure you'll be okay here alone after this news?"

"I've been alone for a long time." Belle smoothed the front of her gown. "I can handle it."

"Okay." He kissed her on the mouth before turning to leave. "I'll call you later."

Belle attempted a smile but didn't have the strength to see it through. She had a father. One who'd been nearby all along. What was it with parents abandoning their kids around here?

HARLAN CALLED LYDIA on the way to Dylan's and told her about Belle's fall and her decision to stay on the ranch. He omitted the fainting episode and the father revelation. Then he called the nursing home to check on Trudy and update them on Belle's condition. By the time they arrived back at the ranch Belle's animals were long overdue on their feedings. Ivy fed them their bottles while Harlan treated Lillie's sunburn. Imogene and Olive ate and curled up together in their stall, but he couldn't in good conscience leave behind the piglet and the lamb.

Together, he and Ivy filled a small kiddie pool with fresh hay and dragged it across the yard and into the house. In hindsight, they should have filled it after they brought it inside. It just fit in the front mudroom. Nobody ever used that door anyway.

After the addition of a few baby gates and checking in with Belle again, he finally had a chance to sit down and try to locate Judge Sanders. He still didn't believe it. And he wasn't so sure Belle should either. There was only one way to find out and that was to ask the man. Five phone calls later, he had the county clerk's phone number. She must know how to reach the judge at home. Harlan looked at his watch. It was half past eight. Still early enough to call.

The phone rang twice before she answered. "Hi, this is Deputy Sheriff Harlan Slade. It's imperative I reach Judge Sanders tonight. Would you happen to have a number for him or could you contact him for me?"

"I can call him and relay the information. May I ask what this is regarding?"

"It's an urgent matter regarding Belle Barnes."

Within minutes, an incoming call came in from an unknown number. "Harlan Slade," he answered.

"Harlan, it's Beckett Sanders. I received a call about Miss Barnes. Or should I call her Mrs. Slade." The man chuckled.

How about calling her daughter?

"She's still going by Barnes." At least that's how he registered her at the hospital today. "Belle had an accident earlier at the nursing home. She requests to see you right away."

"Is she okay?"

"She has a concussion. She said to tell you the matter is extremely urgent."

"Is she in county?"

"Hospital, not jail." Harlan felt the need to clarify that statement. They were talking about Belle after all. He gave the judge the room number and then phoned Belle with an update. He wished he could be there with her when she found out the truth, but she had been right. He belonged with Ivy tonight.

Harlan walked in the living room and found his daughter watching cartoons and Elvis, Samson and Lillie curled up sound asleep beside her.

"Ivy, how did they get out of their pen?"

"I took them out. Elvis was lonely."

Of course he was. He mentally tabulated how much it would cost to get animal poop out of the area rug, because sooner or later, one of the three would spring a leak. Then he remembered the extra shower curtain liner he had in the upstairs bathroom. A few minutes later, the crisis had been averted. If they stayed on the plastic, everyone would remain happy.

"Daddy?"

"Yes, sweetheart?"

"When can I see my mommy?"

A flaming ball of barbed wire hitting him at warp speed would've been preferable over the gnawing ache churning in the pit of his stomach. "Have you slept on it?"

"Yes."

"And you're sure."

"Yes."

"Can you give me more than one-word answers and tell me how you're feeling?"

"I thought about how sad I would be if I never met

you." She flopped against him on the couch. "I don't want to be sad for not knowing Mommy."

That was more deductive reasoning then he'd given her credit for. "I can call her and set up something for this week."

"Can I meet her now?"

"Ivy, it's almost time for bed." She didn't argue. She just stared up at him with those big blue eyes and he was putty in her hands. "Okay, you win. I'll call her and see if she wants to come over tonight. I can't make any promises." He should at least let Molly know Belle wouldn't make their coffee date tomorrow morning.

Harlan was an idiot for doubting Molly would rush straight over. He greeted her on the porch first and warned her that the visit would be brief. "I mean it, Molly. A half hour at the most. She needs to get to bed."

The last time the three of them were in the same house together, it was the day she walked out on them. Molly followed him through the house and into the living room.

"You'll have to ignore the temporary animal play area. I brought the menagerie in while Belle is in the hospital."

Harlan watched Molly's eyes as she took in her surroundings. Instead of zeroing in on Ivy, she noticed everything else about the room, floor to ceiling.

"You changed the place."

Harlan nodded from the doorway. He hadn't allowed her past the kitchen the other day. Her voice was quieter tonight, almost as if she didn't want to attract Ivy's attention.

"Barnyard animals are okay in the house?"

"I took the necessary precautions." Harlan sighed. Belle had been a better mother to his daughter. Molly had been in the house for five minutes and she still hadn't focused on Ivy. "Maybe this was a mistake," Harlan said under his breath.

"Why?" she shot back in a whisper.

"Because that's your daughter. The one you haven't seen in six years, yet you're worried about paint colors and a piglet."

Ivy turned around and stared at Molly. Harlan willed the woman to say something, but she remained silent.

"Ivy, sweetheart." He sat on the floor and pulled her into his lap. "This is Molly. She's your mommy, but you can call her Molly if you want." Molly's narrowed stare didn't faze him. "Remember what I told you the other day? You only do or say what you're comfortable with. Do you want to talk to her?"

Ivy nodded and they both looked up at Molly, who remained on the other side of the room.

"Molly, this won't work unless you're an active participant."

She entered the room and sat on the edge of the couch, as far away as possible. Okay, she wasn't going to come to them and Harlan had promised not to force Ivy. Now what? Harlan eased Ivy onto her feet and he joined Molly on the couch, leaving plenty of room on either side of him for Ivy if she decided to come closer. Instead she sat crossed-legged on the floor in front of them. Elvis crawled into her lap and she proceeded to scratch him behind his ears, never breaking eye contact with Molly.

"My daddy said you wanted to meet me."

"I do. I—I did," Molly stammered. "I can't believe how much you've grown. You're a big girl."

"Do you know my birthday?" Ivy asked.

Harlan had wondered the same thing over the years, considering she had never bothered to send a card.

"May 7."

"How come you never came to see me before?"

"I have seen you before." Molly leaned forward and rested her elbows on her knees. "I lived here with you for the first year of your life. You were just too young to remember."

"You lived in the house with Daddy?" Ivy asked.

Molly side-glanced at him in annoyance. Harlan hadn't seen the need to tell Ivy anything about Molly when she so eagerly renounced custody.

"I did, when your daddy and I were married."

"Like Belle and Daddy are married?"

Molly nodded. "Exactly."

Harlan coughed. The two marriages were more different than a mare and a doorknob.

"Did you live in the stables, too?" Ivy asked.

"I'm sorry. Did I what? Live in the stables? No, I lived in this house with your father."

"Ivy." Harlan shook his head. There was a piece of information Molly didn't need to know.

Molly shifted on the couch. "What does she mean… live in the stables? You and Belle came out of there the other morning. Are you all living in there?"

"Only Belle does," Ivy answered. "Daddy says they only had a pretend wedding because Belle's grandma is sick."

Molly started to laugh. "Oh, that's rich. So what was that the other day? A little booty call?"

"Molly!" Harlan warned. "First, don't disparage my wife, and yes, Molly, she is my legal wife in every sense of the word. And second, don't use that language around my daughter."

"Our daughter," she corrected. "I'm sure she doesn't know what I meant."

"And I'm sure she repeats things she hears even when she shouldn't." Harlan shot Ivy a warning glare.

"Belle reads me bedtime stories." Ivy scooted closer.

"Speaking of bedtime, you need to get ready for yours. But we need to take these three for a walk first. Do you remember where we put all their leashes?" Harlan hadn't been able to find a collar for Samson, so he borrowed an extra one from Elvis. He had noticed Belle never left their collars on like he left on Elvis's and figured she had her reasons.

Ivy returned a few seconds later with all three leashes and two collars. The animals firmly secured, he picked up Samson and Lillie while Ivy walked Elvis to the door on his leash. He stopped halfway onto the porch and called into the living room. "Come on, Molly. That means you, too."

He wasn't about to leave her alone in his house, not even for a second. And their half hour was almost over. Molly trudged to the door. "I thought we'd talk some more."

"Nope." Harlan waited for her to exit before closing the screen door behind them. "Some other time. This was a start."

"Would you like me to read you a bedtime story?"

Molly squatted down beside Ivy. "I'd love to see your room."

Now she'd pushed him too far.

"No, thank you," Ivy said, shutting her down before he even had a chance.

Good girl.

Chapter Twelve

Belle understood why she didn't own a television. She'd scanned the channels with the remote at least a dozen times and nothing captured her interest. It was almost nine thirty and she began to doubt Judge Sanders would show tonight.

A bouquet of flowers appeared in the doorway, causing her to smile. "Harlan, you shouldn't have. I told you to stay home with Ivy."

The man lowered the flowers, uncovering his face. *Judge Sanders*.

"Those are beautiful. Thank you, Dad."

He almost dropped the vase on the roll-away table at the foot of her bed.

"I'm sorry. Too soon?" Belle asked. He paled, almost matching the color of his platinum hair. And for the first time in her life, she wondered whose side of the family her coloring came from. "You do know what I'm referring to, don't you?"

"If you're talking about my relationship with your mother, then yes. But, I'm sorry. I'm not your father. I fear you don't have all the facts."

"I have more facts than you think I do." The more

she ran over the story in her head, the less far-fetched it became. "The timeline fits. After my mother told my grandparents she was pregnant, my grandfather had a heart attack and died. I've already double-checked the date of his death and it is eight months before I was born, which adds credibility to the story. I'm still trying to figure out if my mom ran away from the guilt she carried over my grandfather's death or if my grandmother threw her out."

"I don't understand."

"Grammy fades in and out of decades courtesy of her damned disease, and today she told me she held my mom responsible for her husband's death." Belle steeled her nerves in preparation for the validity of her paternity claim. The mystery surrounding her father had been such a strong part of her life, she wondered if she'd miss it once it was gone. "How much time passed between when my grandparents told you my mom's real age and my grandfather's death?"

Beckett settled in the chair next to the bed before responding. "It was the same day."

Grammy had left that part out. Evidently, she had left out and hidden quite a bit of information. "Did my mom tell you she was pregnant that day?"

"No. I found out she'd had a child after she had abandoned you in Texas." He stared down at his hands in his lap. "By the time you came back to town, I was thirty-three and married. My wife was aware of my past with your mother." His eyes met hers. "I had every intention of pursuing a paternity test, until your grandmother told me the circumstances surrounding Cindy's pregnancy. Let's just say it painted your mom in a rather risqué light and she feared a custody case would follow you around in such a small town. You were having such a hard time of it already. I asked for a private paternity test instead and she refused. My wife and I were more than willing to help support you. We were unable to have children of our own and you would have been welcome in our home. But your grandmother's adamancy led me to strongly believe I wasn't your father. I never had any proof you were mine."

"Well, we can get proof now. We're in a hospital and I want a paternity test. Tonight. You're a county judge. You can make it happen. This small town has been talking about me since I was six years old. Let them talk. I have a thick skin. After twenty-seven years, don't we both deserve the truth?"

"Okay."

"Okay? You mean it's that simple? I don't have to fight you for it?"

"Of course not." Beckett stood and reached for her hand, giving it a gentle squeeze. "I want to know just as much as you do. Let me go track down a nurse and when I get back you can explain how you wound up in the hospital."

Belle watched him leave, and for a moment, she feared he wouldn't return. It wasn't as if he could hide from her. She'd be in front of him again in a few weeks for Lillie's case. Or would she? That was a terrifying thought. If Judge Sanders really was her father, another judge would have to hear her case. Possibly a sterner judge who might try to make an example out of her.

Until she had definitive proof Beckett was her father, she had to ignore the millions of questions running through her head. She stood on the fine line between elation and apprehension. The possibility alone had already contorted her sensibilities. How much more would the truth change?

HARLAN DROPPED IVY off at school on his way to the hospital. Ivy had wanted to see Belle, but she'd already missed enough school. He'd talked to her last night after Judge Sanders had left and she'd sounded down that they had to wait until morning for the paternity-test results.

She'd asked him to bring her a change of clothes from the ranch. She was determined to escape the confines of the hospital today. She'd said it gave her a new appreciation for what her grandmother experienced daily.

He'd originally gone up to her apartment to retrieve what she'd asked for, but the more he'd looked around, the more aggravated he'd become. He refused to have another *you stay in your space and I'll stay in mine* argument when she came home from the hospital. He'd looked up concussions last night and one of the mandatory treatments was plenty of rest. He'd been a complete jerk for allowing her to stay up there as long as she had. Even Molly had recognized it wasn't right, despite Belle's protests. Starting today, she was living in the main house. If she felt more comfortable staying in her own room, she was welcome to use the guest bedroom. Either way, her days of living above the horses were officially over.

Harlan hated hospitals. Being a deputy sheriff meant

seeing the inside of them more than most people. And it was never for a good reason. The scent of the wild-flower bouquet he carried helped mask the astringent smell of the hallway. It had been a long time since he'd bought her flowers. He hoped they were still her favorite.

"Good morning, beautiful." Harlan entered her room, surprised to see Judge Sanders and a woman standing next to Belle's bed.

"Good morning." Despite her surroundings, Belle appeared much better than she had yesterday.

"These are for you." He handed her the bouquet, then looked around for a place to put them.

"Thank you." She lowered her head to sniff the blooms. "I can't believe you remembered." She inhaled deeply. "Harlan, you already know Judge Sanders."

"Please, call me Beckett." The man held out his hand to Harlan and they shook. "This is my wife, Becky."

Harlan was taken slightly aback. Beckett and Becky? You couldn't have planned that even if you tried. "It's a pleasure to meet you, ma'am."

"You, too. I hear you have quite a political future ahead of you. I'd like to talk to you about that some time."

"I do?" Harlan looked at Belle, who shrugged. "You would?"

"My wife has managed more than a few successful political campaigns. You've come up in conversation during various events. I can see you easily running for and winning the sheriff's seat in the near future."

"Wow, thank you. That's my goal." Harlan reached for Belle's hand. "Any word on your test results?"

"I have them right here," a lab technician said from the doorway. "Would you like me to read them?"

"Yes, please." Belle squeezed Harlan's hand tighter.

"Beckett Sanders, you are Belle Barnes's father."

Belle buried her face in her hands and sobbed. Harlan wrapped his arms around her and rocked her gently. "Shh. It's all over now. You finally have your answers." Her body shook and Harlan feared she'd set off an alarm on one of the monitors attached to her. He looked across the bed to Beckett sobbing in his wife's arms.

"I can't believe it. I should have insisted on this test when you were six years old. I am so sorry you had to wait this long. We've lost so much time."

Belle lifted her head. "Can I call you Dad?"

"Of course you can. You can call me anything you'd like." Beckett gave her a hug as Harlan stepped away from the bed.

Becky gestured toward the doorway and they both slipped into the hall unnoticed. "I thought they could use a little privacy. Can I buy you a cup of coffee?" she asked.

"Only if you let me do the buying," Harlan said.

"You have a deal. I heard you have a daughter of your own."

"Ivy. She's seven, in a remarkably similar situation as Belle."

"How so?" Becky asked as they stepped into the elevator.

Over the next half hour and two cups of ultrastrong coffee, he explained his situation with Molly to Becky. The woman was easy to talk to. He'd never had that type of relationship with his mom. His dad had always been his go-to guy, and he'd missed him even more than normal during the past week.

"Beckett feels an enormous amount of guilt for Belle's—how shall I phrase it—police record I guess is the best choice. It will always hang over him. Had he been a father to her, would she have made the same choices?"

"I can answer that." Harlan nodded. "She would have. Who raised her wouldn't have affected her passion. Then again, maybe not." He sagged against the back of the cafeteria chair. "Maybe she would have become an animal rights attorney instead. Either way, she'd be involved in animal rights. Her first instinct is to protect the weak. Animals, the elderly, children. She's a protector."

"It's sweet the way you talk about her. She's a lucky woman. And your daughter's lucky to have a father willing to accept her mother back into her life."

"More like tolerate. Molly and Ivy didn't take well to each other last night. The first time Ivy met Belle, she was all over her. And Belle loves every second of it. But she's afraid Ivy will feel she needs to choose either her or Molly. I want to tell her it's okay to have two moms but I'm having a hard time accepting Molly as her mother. Belle yes, Molly not so much."

"You need to get over that," Becky said matter-of-factly. "You're allowing your feelings toward Molly to taint your daughter. Kids pick up on the tension. If she senses you are uncomfortable, she'll follow your lead. That's why a lot of supervised visitation is overseen by a neutral party. It gives the child a chance to develop their own thoughts and feelings about the person."

Harlan hadn't considered his terseness toward Molly might have influenced Ivy last night. She would have been better off with his uncle Jax supervising. That man had never met another human or animal he didn't like.

"You've given me a lot to think about. Thank you for listening."

"Hey, don't mention it." She patted his hand. "We're family now."

"I guess we are." He tapped his cup on the table and smiled. "What do you say? Think we've given them enough time?"

"They're going to need a lifetime." Becky rose and slung her purse over her shoulder. "We're the ones that will need to adjust to sharing them with other people."

And that meant sharing Ivy with Molly. He would do it to spare her the pain Belle suffered her entire life. He'd do anything for the people he loved.

ALL BELLE WANTED to do was take a long hot shower, check on her babies and sleep for the rest of the day. Harlan parked the truck almost on top of the fence behind the house.

"You wait right there." He hopped out and ran to the passenger-side door before she had a chance to touch the door handle. "Give me your hand."

"Harlan." She smacked it away. "Stop it before you drive me insane."

"The doctor said you needed plenty of rest."

He held her elbow as if she were an elderly woman crossing the street. Arguing didn't work, so she allowed him to continue his smothering. "You can help me up to my apartment, and then I'll be fine. You need to get to work anyway."

"I moved you into the house this morning."

"You did what?" Belle forced a tight smile. "I mean, that was nice of you, but you didn't have to do that. I really need the peace and quiet, and the stables are peaceful and quiet."

"It's too cold, too damp, you just got out of the hospital and it doesn't even have a proper kitchen. You can't even fix anything to eat unless it fits in that Barbie-size refrigerator up there. And before you protest some more, I set you up in the guest room. I figured you'd still want your own space."

He was setting her up in the exact situation he told her she wouldn't like if she stayed at Lydia's. That made sense.

"You're not happy, are you?" He frowned.

"I feel icky and tired. Once I get past that, we will be good to go. I'll do that while you're at work, because you are going to work."

Once they were inside and she'd gotten over the initial shock of Samson and Lillie residing in Harlan's mudroom, she sank deep into the claw-foot tub, allowing the water to engulf her in a cocoon of warmth. She heard Harlan's truck drive away and exhaled the deepest breath she felt like she'd held since her grandmother mentioned Judge Sanders. Correction. Her father.

"Father." Belle wrinkled her nose. It sounded too formal.

"Dad." It was short, sweet and to the point. It had possibilities.

"Daddy." Too Ivy. She laughed.

"Pa." She cringed. "Papa. That sounds like a steam engine."

"Pop." She pursed her lips. Bubble Wrap pops; people don't.

The only one that sounded good to her was Dad.

"Dad." She tested the word again. How did little kids make this decision? That was stressful. Belle never had the opportunity to use the word. Harlan's father had been a part of her life since she moved to Saddle Ridge, and she had called him Mr. Slade.

Discovering her father was a bigger relief than most people could fathom. When you don't know who one or both of your parents are, your mind begins to play tricks on you. When you meet someone who resembles you in some way, you wonder if you're related. When you're dating, or considering going out with the cute guy across the room, you wonder if he could be your brother or maybe a cousin. A million what-ifs follow you around every day, wherever you go. It's exhausting. You don't even realize you're doing it, until you find yourself nursing your drink alone at the end of a bar.

One test result wiped those fears out of her life for good. She may not have any siblings, but she had cousins, aunts, uncles and grandparents. Why the secrecy? Belle had asked her grandmother numerous times about her father when she was younger. Trudy had always claimed not to know. It wasn't like Beckett had some nefarious past. The community respected him. Maybe Trudy thought his family would replace her, even though nobody could. She should have had more faith in Belle. At least she'd unearthed some of the answers that had plagued her all her life. Now she'd never have to worry about being alone again.

Belle stepped out of the tub when the water had cooled and wrapped herself in a giant bath sheet. "Score one for Harlan." The man had impeccable taste in towels.

She rummaged through her clothes and found nothing comfortable enough. She didn't own much and what she did was on the tighter side. Harlan's bedroom door stood open across the hall. She padded into the room and looked around. Steel-gray walls, white trim, minimal furniture. The palette was neutral and could lean a little more gender neutral with the right accents.

"Let's see what you have that's comfortable to wear." She eased open the closet and stepped inside. A pair of police academy sweatpants and a T-shirt sat on the top shelf. She reached for them and gave them a quick sniff test. They were clean. She slipped out of her towel and hung it on the doorknob. The cotton of the shirt against her bare skin instantly soothed her. She pulled on the pants and tied them at the waist. They were oversize and ridiculously comfy.

Her body begged for sleep. Suddenly the other bedroom seemed a million miles away. She tugged at the comforter and crawled under the covers. Harlan's raw scent engulfed her.

Now, this was home.

Chapter Thirteen

"Happy two-week anniversary, sweetheart," Harlan whispered in her ear.

"Mmm." Belle stretched languidly beneath the toasty warm covers. "Am I in your bed?" Her mind tried to retrace her steps. The last thing she remembered was taking a bath. "Have I been asleep since I got home from the hospital?"

"Well, you did get up a few times to use the bathroom," Harlan said. "But other than that, yes, you have been sleeping. It was exactly what the doctor ordered."

"I have to get up. What time is it?" She squinted to read the clock on Harlan's side of the bed. "Did you sleep here with me? Harlan, what if Ivy came in?"

"Relax. I slept in the other room." Harlan stood and pulled a uniform shirt from his closet. "Lydia knows you won't be at work for the next few days, the animals have already been fed, the stalls have been mucked, Ivy's almost ready to get on the school bus and I'm heading into work."

"I could get used to this."

"I hope you do." He attempted to kiss her, before she turned away.

"Yuck." Belle covered her mouth with the sheet. "I have morning breath. If I slept for that long, I probably have more than morning breath."

Harlan grinned down at her. "You look good wearing my clothes," he said as he fastened his uniform shirt cuffs.

"Sorry. I raided your closet. I didn't have anything comfortable."

"No need to apologize. I'm glad me and my things make you feel that way. I was pleasantly surprised to find you asleep in my bed."

"That was comfortable, too." Belle rolled onto her side and hugged his pillow. "And it smells like you."

Harlan laughed. "Some people are offended by that smell." He sat on the edge of the bed. "You might want to stay upstairs for a little while longer, though."

"Why?"

"Because Molly is downstairs eating breakfast with Ivy."

"Oh. When did that happen?" Belle sat up and leaned against the headboard. Surprisingly her head didn't hurt.

"After speaking with Becky yesterday while you and your father got to know each other better, I realized I had been projecting my anger toward Molly onto Ivy. She was defending me in her own little way. I need to give her a chance to form her own opinions about Molly without any interference. That's why they are downstairs and I'm here waking you up. It gives them some time alone without them being completely unsupervised."

"That's a good idea."

"Molly will only be in town for another week. She has a life and job to return to. She hasn't decided if she wants to move back here or stay in Billings. She and Ivy will need many more visits before she makes any of those decisions."

"Have you given any thought to visitation?"

"No." Harlan rose from the bed, effectively ending that line of questioning. "I wanted to run something by you, but I don't want you to feel obligated."

Belle slid back down the bed and pulled the covers over her head. "Do I even want to know?"

"Since you couldn't make your coffee date with Molly yesterday, I wondered if you wanted her to stay after Ivy and I left. It would give you two a chance to talk. If not, I will push her out the door when I leave."

Belle groaned. Molly wasn't her ideal way to start the day, but they had to have a conversation at some point. She flung aside the covers.

"When are you leaving?"

"Twenty minutes."

"Okay, that gives me enough time to shower."

Belle grabbed a change of clothes from the guest room and dragged herself into the bathroom. She already felt tired and she hadn't even done anything yet. She wasn't sure if it was from oversleeping or her concussion. Either way, she didn't like having to choose Molly over bed.

She made it downstairs with a few minutes to spare. "Good morning, sweet pea." Belle pressed a kiss to the top of Ivy's head. "Good morning, Molly." Belle grinned as politely as she could before coffee. She poured a cup and sat down next to Ivy. "Your daddy told me you've become an amazing rescue-animal care-taker. I appreciate all of your help."

"Would you like me to fix you something to eat before I leave?" Harlan asked.

"No, thank you. I'll make something later." At least she'd kept her promise not to dine with Molly. If anyone had told her they'd be sitting across the table from one another during this century, she'd have pushed them into Flathead Lake.

"So, Molly." Either the milk was sour or the other woman's name left a bad taste in her mouth. "We didn't get a chance to talk yesterday. Do you want to stick around for a little bit after they leave?"

"Sure." Molly's face brightened. "I'd like that."

"I don't want to go to school." Ivy rested her head against Belle's arm. "I want to stay home and take care of you."

"Sweetie, I'm okay." Belle wrapped her arm around Ivy's small shoulders and gave her a light squeeze. "They wouldn't have released me if I wasn't." Belle glanced up and saw Molly watching them longingly. She wished she didn't understand what she was feeling, but she did. It was the same look Belle used to get when she watched other kids with their parents. Being an outsider sucked and despite the bad blood between then, Molly's pain bothered her.

"Come on, pumpkin." Harlan reached for Ivy's hand. "It's time to go."

"Bye, Belle." Ivy gave her a hug. "Take care of Elvis for me today."

"I will, sweetheart."

"Bye, Molly," Ivy said, keeping the table between her and her mother. "Come on, Dad. You're slow."

"I'll see you later." Harlan bent over and gave Belle a full kiss on the mouth. "Mmm. Minty."

Heat rose to Belle's cheeks before she realized Molly had been studying her. *Awkward.*

"How are you feeling?" Molly sounded genuine enough, but Belle wondered if Molly secretly wished she'd disappear.

"Better, thank you."

"What happened? Harlan said you fell at the nursing home."

Belle snickered. "Let me tell you something about those nursing home floors. They're hard. Like bust-your-head-open hard. Now I understand why there are so many broken hips in those places. It knocked me out cold. According to Harlan, Grammy said my head bounced like a basketball." Belle grabbed the coffeepot from the counter and topped both her and Molly's mugs. She snatched a doughnut on the way back to the table. As long as it didn't involve an eating utensil, it didn't count as a meal in her book. "I didn't fall. I fainted."

Belle hadn't officially decided how much of the story she would tell Molly, but given her situation with Ivy, she thought it might help.

"Are you sick?" Molly whispered and reached across the table for her hands.

Belle stared down at the all-too-personal contact. "I'm not sick."

"Whew." Molly sat back. "That's good."

Belle saw genuine concern in her former friend's

eyes. "Grammy has her lucid and not-so-lucid moments. Yesterday afternoon, she had regressed back to when I was ten years old. She asked me if I had seen me in the hallway. It was a very surreal moment. I had to talk about myself in third person. I don't know who she thought I was—one of the nurses, perhaps—but she started talking about my mom and my grandfather."

"Your grandfather died before you were born, right?"

"Right. Turns out Grammy knew who my father was all along, and the revelation of my mom's pregnancy is what gave my grandfather a heart attack and killed him."

"No." Molly pulled her chair closer to the table. "You asked her repeatedly if she knew."

"Well, now I know. When she told me, the news literally knocked me off my feet. And that's how I got my concussion."

"I can't believe it." Molly's hand flew to her cheek. "What are you going to do now? Track him down?"

"There's no tracking him down."

"Oh, don't tell me he's dead."

"Nope, Dad is alive and well. He only lives a few miles away."

"Had you heard of him before?"

Belled nodded. She didn't know how much Molly knew about her police record and even though it was available to the public, Belle preferred the less-is-best approach.

"He's an acquaintance."

"That was one of your worst fears."

"We confirmed his paternity yesterday when I was

in the hospital, but we haven't discussed when or how we'll tell people we're related. We're in the getting-to-know-you stage and it's awkward, yet comforting in the same respect. Do you understand what I'm trying to say?"

"It's not very different from me and Ivy."

"Exactly. I can relate to your situation from Ivy's point of view. She's very cautious and she tends to mull over various scenarios in her head before she acts. And I think that's what she's doing with you, based on what Harlan told me. I'm a jump first, then worry if there's water in the pool type of person. Ivy wants to know how much water's in the pool, the type of water and the temperature before she jumps. She's very thorough."

"She definitely gets that from Harlan," Molly said. "My rarely think mentality has gotten me in more trouble."

"Do you have any other kids?" Belle asked.

Molly smiled. "I had my tubes tied the day Ivy was born. I didn't see children in my future back then."

"What's changed?"

"Therapy, for one. I didn't bond with Ivy when she was born. There was something missing and when I look back on it now, I should have sought help. I may have had a touch of postpartum depression. I didn't talk to anyone about it until last year. I just ran and kept moving. I've traveled to every continent and more countries than I can count. I love my job with the travel agency, but despite what Harlan or anyone else thinks, I didn't forget about my daughter. I did her a favor because I would have made her life miserable if I had stayed."

"I had wondered if that was why you left."

"I wasn't happy when I got pregnant. I was jealous of you. You were getting what you wanted. A family with Harlan. It was an obtainable goal for you. All you two had to do was walk down the aisle. Who knew Harlan would get cold feet? When I ran into him at the bar that night, I didn't have some master plan to destroy your life. We drank too much, we shared our fears and we made a bad decision. And I'm sure in the back of my mind I was thinking that by sleeping with Harlan I'd destroy your dream forever. Honestly, I didn't even remember it had happened. My only proof was Ivy."

"Is that supposed to make me feel better?" She'd heard both sides, but a betrayal was just that…a betrayal, and no lame excuse changed it. It still bothered her, but her heart no longer ached over it. She'd forgiven Harlan. Molly not so much. Not yet. "Why did you marry him, then? You didn't love him."

"I didn't love myself either. I was scared and alone. Raising a child was terrifying enough. Raising a child alone multiplied that fear exponentially. I'm sorry my actions hurt you. You were the one person who was always kind to me. I was the outcast kid."

"I wasn't exactly Miss Popular."

"But Harlan was," they both said in unison.

"Yeah, he was, wasn't he?" Belle hadn't considered Harlan popular back then. He played football and rode on the high school rodeo circuit, but he'd always been her boy friend and that had naturally progressed into him being her actual boyfriend.

"People notice you when you're with Harlan. You're

married to him now. Tell me you didn't see a shift in how people treat you."

If Molly's theory was true, she cringed to think how people would treat her once they learned Judge Sanders was her father. "I think it's negligible now versus back then. We were nineteen."

"I see the way Ivy looks at you. She's already attached."

"If anything, she may be a little starstruck or mesmerized because I'm new in her father's life and I come with baby animals. But I adore her and I'll do anything to protect her from—"

"Go ahead, you can say it. You want to protect her from me."

"I want you to be the mother she deserves. I don't want her to go through the hell I went through."

"You're one of the reasons I came back. I didn't want her to turn into you."

Belle pushed her chair from the table. "Are you kidding me?"

Molly buried her face in her hands. "That came out all wrong." Molly wiped her eyes. "I meant I didn't want her to suffer and wonder the way you had. That's why I'm here. And for the record, I'm sorry Alzheimer's is robbing you of your grandmother. That must make finding your father all the more bittersweet."

Belle stared into her coffee mug. She wanted to hate the woman across the table from her, but Molly had stepped back into her life and seemingly understood what she was going through without Belle having to explain it.

"My outlook on life is very different now. I didn't

see my grandmother at all yesterday because I was in the hospital. She saw me faint and called for help. She didn't recognize me when it happened, so while she may have that memory stored, it's not associated with me. I must see her today. It's like *Wheel of Fortune*. Every time I walk in there, I'm spinning the wheel to see which year we'll land on. I would love to ask her why she kept my father from me. He even confronted her because he wanted to provide for me, but she refused. What was she protecting me from? I will never know. But I've learned life is too short to worry about it. Take every opportunity you have to spend time with Ivy. Give her a chance to get to know you. Do you feel I am in the way of your progress with her?"

"It's difficult watching you bond with her," Molly admitted. "But you're fulfilling the role I couldn't. When I came here, I hadn't counted on competing for my daughter's attention. I thought I was entitled to it. You're sitting here telling me about your father and you two seem to have hit it off because you're related. It's an instant bond. Ivy's still not bonding with me. It was similar to the way she reacted to me as a baby. She didn't look me in the eyes or want me to hug her. It didn't help no one was around to show me how to be a mother. My parents provided for me while I was growing up but they never showed any affection. It wasn't as if I could ask them for help. I should have taken the parenting classes at the hospital, but I didn't. Harlan brought me home from the hospital and went to work, leaving me alone to feed, change and take care of a newborn baby."

"I can't imagine how difficult that must have been."

"When Ivy had colic, that's when I realized I couldn't be her mother. She cried all the time. She needed love and affection and nothing I did made it better. And this ranch is so isolated. I get the appeal, but when you're a young clueless mom, you need other moms around."

Belle had a newfound respect for Molly's decision to walk away. You hear horrifying stories on the news about parents trying to kill their children. If more of them walked away and left them with a responsible caretaker, maybe there wouldn't be so many stories.

She also realized for the first time that Harlan hadn't been completely blameless.

"How would you like to do me a favor?"

"Um, sure."

"I'm not allowed to drive for a few days. Could you drop me off at the nursing home?"

"Do you need me to wait around?"

"No. Harlan can give me a ride home later. I'll meet you outside in a minute."

"Belle," Molly said from the porch door. "For what it's worth, I admire the little family you and Harlan have created. I'm glad Ivy has two people who know how to care for her."

Belle set their mugs in the sink and ran water in them. "Thank you, Molly. That's one of the best compliments I've ever received."

Chapter Fourteen

It was Saturday morning and Harlan couldn't believe how calm and peaceful their week had been. Belle's concussion had kept her on the ranch and out of trouble. She had spent her days between the nursing home and speaking with people in various county offices trying to gather the paperwork for her nonprofit rescue center. Harlan was surprised by how many forms she had to fill out and how many hoops she would need to jump through before she would be able to open her doors. Beckett had even taken an interest in the project and helped Belle understand all the legalities. Her plans, while simple, allowed the operation to grow with provisions for future satellite locations. He gave her a lot of credit. When she wasn't working to rehabilitate the animals, she was trying to find ways to save them.

Harlan flipped a pancake in the air to Ivy's enthusiastic applause. Belle had her head buried in her laptop and Molly was still trying to find a connection with their daughter. Ivy had shown some effort, but she had become more bonded with Belle. Molly was leaving on Monday, but Harlan reassured her that she could return anytime and continue to grow her relationship with Ivy. Their family—however unconventional—had begun to function smoothly. There was only one problem. He and Belle were in a perpetual state of limbo. The last time they had really kissed had been almost a week ago. They had become roommates instead of the married couple he wanted them to be. He'd hoped there would have been some improvement by now, but she kept him at arm's length. The tension had dissipated but it wasn't enough. Not for him.

After breakfast, Harlan asked Belle to take a walk with him while Molly spent some time alone with Ivy.

"This is a nice surprise." Belle entwined her fingers in his and rested her head on his shoulder as they strolled down the ranch drive. "We never have any time alone together."

Harlan looked skyward and shook his head. "Are you saying you want to be alone with me?"

Belle stopped walking and faced him. "I'm saying I want to see where this goes. I've spent the last week around you and Molly. I can see there's no love lost between the two of you. I trust you're not going to ditch me because of her again. I was going to ask you out on a date once she went back to Billings. But since we're alone, now's good." Belle cupped his face and drew her down to him. "I want to be with you, in every way."

Harlan gathered her to him and pressed his mouth to hers, feeling the fervent heat of her desire. The love in his heart surged through every ounce of his being. Belle Barnes wanted to be his wife and he had to show her how much she meant to him. He broke their kiss and gazed deep in her eyes. "I need you more than I've ever needed anyone. And I need you now."

Harlan didn't wait for her to reply. He laced his fingers in hers and began running toward the stables. Once inside and away from prying eyes, he lifted Belle into his arms as her legs wrapped around his waist. She grabbed his face and kissed him, harder, deeper than before.

"Make love to your wife," she whispered against his mouth.

Harlan groaned, climbing the stairs faster than he thought possible. He set her on the bed and smiled. Belle was meant to be savored, and he planned on enjoying every inch of her.

MOLLY'S RAUCOUS COUGHING downstairs woke them from their postcoital slumber. Harlan heard voices coming from the outside stable and checked his watch. *Crap!* They'd forgotten Becky and Beckett were coming over to discuss the possible location of various rescue center buildings.

Harlan quickly dressed and peered down the stable stairs.

"Will you hurry up already!" Molly whispered loudly. "I told them you went out for a ride. Get yourself together and I'll get them to meet you on the other side of the ranch."

A half hour later, they'd paced off numerous sites. They were just waiting on Belle's licenses to come through before he transferred the land to her name. The one drawback to the other side of the ranch was the close proximity to other residences. Belle didn't want her rescue to lower their property values or impact their lives in any way. That meant changing her plans and running the rescue center deeper into the property instead of across the front as she had originally planned.

There was still a lot of work to be done before she opened her doors, but the happiness and contentment on her face made him want to support Belle in any way possible. The animals weren't the only ones who deserved a forever home on the ranch.

They had just sat down to dinner when a black SUV pulled down the ranch drive.

"I wonder who that is." Harlan excused himself from the table and stepped onto the porch. A man climbed out and called to him from the gate.

"Do you have a little girl, around seven or eight years old with brown hair?"

"May I ask what this is about?"

"Yeah, I find it real funny how you're supposed to uphold the law, yet your daughter stole from me."

Harlan felt the hair on the back of his neck rise as he descended the stairs and met the man at the gate. "You better have more than words to back up that statement."

"Harlan, is everything okay?" Belle and Beckett waited on the porch.

He held up his hand and faced the man again. "What are you claiming my daughter took from you?"

"My wife saw her steal our rabbit from the hutch in the backyard."

"We have animals but we don't have rabbits," Harlan said.

"She had to put it somewhere."

"When did your wife see this happen?"

"Two hours ago. She has been waiting for me to come home so I could discuss it with you." Harlan didn't like that timeline. Two hours ago they were on the other side of the ranch, very close to one of the neighbor's houses.

"Do you mind waiting here while I talk to my daughter?"

The man nodded and leaned against his SUV.

Harlan bounded up the stairs and into the house. Ivy's frightened stare answered his question before he even questioned her.

"What is going on?" Belle asked.

Ivy slowly pushed her chair away from the table and inched closer to Molly.

"That man out there says two hours ago his wife watched Ivy steal their rabbit out of the hutch in their backyard."

"She wouldn't do that, Harlan." Molly stood, blocking Ivy from his view.

"Molly, with all due respect, I need to talk to my daughter."

"Our daughter."

Belle squeezed past them and ran upstairs. The creaking of the floorboards overhead and the sound of doors being opened and closed announced her presence in every room.

"Ivy, will you please return to your seat."

Ivy slinked back onto her chair and averted her eyes.

"Ivy, where did you put the bunny?" Harlan asked.

Molly threw her hands in the air, clearly exasperated with his choice of words.

"Ivy."

Belle returned downstairs, out of breath, shaking

her head. She tapped Molly on the shoulder. "Excuse me, let me sit there for a second."

Molly huffed and stood next to Beckett and Becky.

"Ivy, sweetheart." Belle held Ivy's hands in hers. "Did you find a hurt bunny?"

Ivy lifted her gaze and met Belle's.

"Did you put it someplace safe where it wouldn't get hurt again?"

Ivy slowly nodded.

Molly gasped, and Harlan uttered a muffled expletive.

"Okay, it's okay." Belle reassured his daughter. She had more patience than he did at the moment. "Will you show me where the bunny is so I can help make it better?"

Ivy stood and led Belle to the porch door. "Is it in the stables?"

Ivy nodded.

"Okay, let's go check on the bunny." Belle turned to face him. "Harlan, can you and my dad pacify that man while I examine this rabbit?"

"Hey! Where are you going?" the man yelled after Belle and Ivy.

"Hey! Don't yell at my wife and kid." Harlan's temper flared. "Don't you forget for one second that I'm a deputy sheriff. And this man here is a county judge. So zip it until we can sort this out."

"There's nothing to sort out," the man spat.

"My daughter indicated the rabbit was sick or injured." Harlan ground his back teeth.

"That rabbit's fine. And it's not sick or injured. It's

fat because my son feeds it too many cookies. Your daughter stole my kid's pet."

Belle emerged from the stables, carrying the rabbit. She met the man at the gate and handed it to him. "I sincerely apologize. She thought because the bunny was in the hutch in the middle of the yard that someone left it there and forgot about it."

He placed the rabbit in the front seat and closed the door without getting in. "This isn't an injured cow in the middle of a cattle ranch."

"How did you—?" Belle scoffed. "You were there that night."

"Yeah, I guess the apple doesn't fall far from the tree. Like mother, like daughter. You're both thieves. No wonder you never go to jail. You got the law in your back pocket."

Harlan's body hardened as he clenched his fists. "Get off my land before I arrest you." Harlan closed the distance between them. "How dare you come onto my ranch and yell at my wife. She has apologized."

"I take it back." Anger lit her eyes as she took a step forward. "A rabbit hutch sitting out in the open like that is bait for wolves, coyotes, bear and other predatory animals."

The man's face reddened. "There you go sticking your nose where it doesn't belong again. Someone needs to teach you a lesson."

"That does it." Harlan spun the man around and slammed him face forward onto the hood of the SUV. No one was going to threaten his family and get away with it. He twisted the man's arm behind his back and held him down. "Belle, go get the handcuffs hanging by the back door."

"You should be handcuffing your wife. She's the thief."

Harlan tightened his grip. Belle ran to him and handed him the cuffs. "You have the right to remain silent," he began as he cuffed and frisked the man before sitting him on the ground. He sent Belle back inside for his badge and keys before tossing the man in the back of his cruiser. Becky offered to drive the bunny and the man's SUV to his wife and Beckett said he'd inform her of her husband's unfortunate overnight incarceration before he met up with Harlan at the station. Nothing like having a judge as your star witness.

Truth be told, Harlan was grateful for the distraction. He needed to cool down before he saw Belle again. He had warned her repeatedly that her actions could affect him or his daughter. Now his daughter was mimicking her. People knew who Belle was because of her record. He didn't want Ivy to suffer the same fate. The situation tonight had been bad enough. Belle made it worse when she verbally attacked the man about his rabbit hutch. Now he had to worry about this guy and his friends coming onto his ranch to teach his wife and kid a lesson. He slammed the steering wheel.

By the time he and Beckett arrived home a few hours later, Molly and Belle were engaged in an ear-splitting screaming match. This did not go on in his house. Molly didn't know how to fight at normal octaves. He always said her goal was to shatter glass.

Harlan bounded up the back stairs and flung open the screen door so hard he knocked it off its hinges.

"Enough! We don't fight like this here. And definitely not in front of my daughter. Where is Ivy?"

"She's upstairs with Becky," Belle said.

"Okay, good. Molly, get out. Belle, don't say another word. I can't deal with either one of you tonight. The two of you are like teenagers again."

"Why didn't you tell me she had a police record a mile long?"

"Because it's none of your business," Belle answered.

"You're living with my daughter. It makes it my business." Molly spun around to face Harlan. "Do you know what our daughter said after you left? She couldn't understand why you were so mad since Belle got arrested all the time and nothing bad happened to her. She even said you had to arrest her last week."

"Oh, dear." Beckett sighed.

"Was that man right? Is that what's going on around here? Belle runs amok stealing animals all in the name of compassion, you arrest her and then her father lets her off? You guys have a great thing going on here. Does the county know about this? What about family services? I think they need to know."

"Whoa, there." Beckett held up his hands. "There's no need to get nasty. You don't have all the facts."

"My daughter told me she sat in a courtroom and listened while Belle was on trial."

"I had her removed from the courtroom as soon as Belle brought her presence to my attention."

"Why was she there?" Molly demanded.

"Because she was spending the day with me at work," Harlan said.

"How did she get into the courthouse?"

"She walked in." Harlan huffed. "I don't appreciate being schooled on parenting by a woman who didn't give a damn for six years."

"I guess you let her run around the courthouse the same way you let her run into a neighbor's yard and steal rabbits. I can't allow Ivy to remain in this environment."

"What are you saying?" Harlan didn't like Molly's implication.

"I will call family services in the morning and then I'll petition the court for full custody of Ivy. I walked away from my daughter to protect her from the bad environment I had created around her. Now Belle is creating the bad environment and you two are enabling her. It's over."

Harlan stormed onto the back porch before he did or said something he would regret. No one would take his daughter from him. He'd sacrifice the world to keep her safe and by his side.

"ARE YOU EVER going to come back in the house?" Belle had never seen Harlan so angry or distant. Not even when he had arrested her. He had been sitting on the back porch steps for over three hours after everyone else had left and Ivy had gone to bed. "I think we should talk about what happened."

"You're right. We should."

That was a start. "Would you like me to put on a pot of coffee?"

"What I have to say won't take that long." Harlan rubbed his palms against the front of his jeans as he stood. "I don't want Ivy to hear us, so can you close the door and come out here, please?"

Belle eased the door shut. She hadn't broken any promises—in fact, she had done everything she could to move forward with her rescue. She was proud of the ground she'd covered and the accomplishments she'd made. She didn't need any more lectures.

"I'm going to have to ask you to leave."

Belle heard the words but they didn't register. She shook her head, trying to break free from the giant cobweb clouding her brain. "You don't mean that."

"I do mean it and I need a divorce sooner than later. I think we're well past an annulment at this point."

The cool tone to his voice froze her heart midbeat.

"Why are you doing this? You asked me to move in and I told you no repeatedly. And then you moved me in while I was in the hospital, much to my chagrin I might add. But I went along with it. And just when I finally say yes you want out?"

"I don't have a choice. On paper, you are a terrible influence on my child. I had to arrest a man on my own property because my daughter was emulating you. And instead of just returning the rabbit and calling it a day, you elevated this situation to the point where this man said you needed to be taught a lesson. A threat against you is a threat against my daughter. Molly was witness to all of it. And to top it off, she can call Beckett as her witness. All of this happened in front of the most credible witness out there. Your dad may have helped you in court before, but he can't save you from this one. He's not going to lie under oath for you. I love you, but we're done."

"Don't you dare tell me that you love me for the first time and then follow it with a *we're done*." Belle's body trembled. "You're like Lucy with the football. You kept taunting and teasing until you got me where you wanted, and then once I'm finally happy, working hard to create a legal business, you're throwing me out? I told you I was moving into Lydia's a week ago and you stopped me. You practically begged me to stay."

"I have full custody of my daughter and at the very best, now they will probably grant me joint. I stand to lose full custody of my daughter. My. Daughter. She might be ripped from the only place she's ever lived, because of your recklessness. And it doesn't matter if you've changed. Your actions have severe consequences and all of us are going to pay for it. Depending on how far Molly takes this, your dad can be removed from the bench. I will probably never make sheriff. But worst of all, Ivy might be thrown in foster care until they can sort this out. You're unbelievable, Belle."

A sob caught in her throat. She never wanted to hurt Ivy. She'd never wanted to disrupt their lives. She had fought, repeatedly. But she had failed, and now there was nothing left.

"I'll be out by the morning."

"I'm sorry, Belle." Harlan's cold, unaffected stare met hers. "I need you to leave tonight."

"It's almost midnight."

"You need to go. The animals can stay until tomorrow, but I can't have you under my roof in case family services shows up. I need every trace of you gone."

His words hit her harder than any fists ever could.

"No." Belle slowly shook her head from side to

side. "I am not coming back here tomorrow. I'll take everything—animals included—tonight. Please pack up the belongings you moved into the house without my permission and leave them on the porch. I need to make a few phone calls. Oh, and don't worry, I won't contest the divorce."

Belle headed toward the stables to call Lydia in private. She'd known moving in with him was a bad idea. The whole situation was bad from the beginning. She should have followed her gut instinct.

She despised herself as much as she despised Harlan. She could have been stronger and remained steadfast. He was right. She'd destroyed all of them and if anything happened to Ivy it was because of her.

She removed her phone from her pocket and dialed Lydia. It was so late and she was bound to wake the kids. She had nowhere else to turn. Under the circumstances, she didn't think Beckett and Becky would welcome her with open arms.

"Belle?" Lydia's sleepy voice answered. "Do you know what time it is?"

"Lydia, I need your help. I'm in trouble."

"Aw hell, Belle."

Chapter Fifteen

Almost two and a half weeks had passed since Harlan had thrown Belle off the ranch and she had moved in with Lydia and her family. His attorney had sent over a joint divorce petition for her to sign along with the title transfer for fifty acres of land. She tore the land transfer in half and tossed it in the trash. Hell would freeze over before she accepted anything from Harlan ever again.

Multiple yellow sign-here flags sticking out from between the petition's pages beckoned mockingly to her. She flipped to the first one and saw Harlan's signature. It shouldn't have surprised her, yet it did in a most hurtful way. How could she have allowed him to break her heart twice?

She wiped at her eyes and jammed the document back in the envelope. She'd have it notarized on her way into town before dropping it back off at the attorney's. The sooner their divorce was official, the better.

First, she needed to finish making her rounds on Lydia's ranch. When her friend refused the rent she offered, Belle said she would work the ranch in exchange for room and board. Lydia agreed and every morning

Belle spent three hours feeding and cleaning up after two barns and one stable full of animals. The woman had taken in more rescues than she had room.

Belle had left Imogene behind for Ivy. Harlan had told her they wanted to adopt the duck. It was the least she could do after uprooting all their lives. Molly hadn't made good on any of her threats. She had returned to Billings until she could find a new position in or around Saddle Ridge and had agreed not to seek custody if Harlan agreed to keep Belle away from Ivy.

Lillie and Samson continued to thrive and were old enough to stay in Lydia's barn along with the other baby animals. And Olive was finally paired with another frostbitten, earless goat. The two had become inseparable. Belle vowed to find each of the animals in their care forever homes, but she knew most of them would end up permanent residents in the rescue center. While it was a satisfactory solution, the animals didn't receive as much one-on-one love and affection as they would in a smaller environment.

Belle longed for the day when work meant stepping out her back door—when her rescues would have the freedom to roam under her watchful eye. That dream had been so close she could have touched it. Having to start over again sucked, but Lydia recently had the opportunity to buy some acreage adjacent to her own ranch. She was just waiting to see if the owner accepted the offer. While it wasn't Belle's ideal vision for the rescue, it would work with some modifications to her business plan. Lydia's support and devotion to the cause gave her hope for the future.

In four days, she would move into her new apartment. Beckett had called to check in on her a few times since that fateful night, but their relationship hadn't been the same. He still maintained contact with Harlan and had tried repeatedly to get them to talk to one another. Even if she wanted to talk to Harlan, Molly had threatened an all-out custody war if he spoke to Belle. She couldn't ask him to take that risk. Their short relationship wasn't worth it.

After Belle had finished her chores she headed into town. The nursing home was her first stop, followed by the feed and grain. Belle had approved her grandmother's move into the quieter Alzheimer's wing. She was still regressing but it seemed to have slowed down somewhat.

The memory train always seemed to stop on major events in Belle's life, not some random moment in time. She wished she had known during each of those moments just how much they would come to mean to her grandmother. It still amazed Belle the level of detail Trudy could recall about one particular event, yet an entire decade had vanished from her mind. Yesterday they had been transported back to Belle's sixteenth birthday. At least that was a time before she had started dating Harlan seriously. Trudy no longer asked for him, but the nurses had told her he stopped in every day at noon and ate lunch with her.

"Good morning," Belle said as she walked past the main desk and headed toward the Alzheimer's wing.

"Excuse me, Mrs. Slade."

Belle froze. "It's Barnes," she said before turning around.

Samantha Frederick smiled meekly. "I'm so sorry

about you and—" Belle's brows rose at the almost mention of Harlan's name. "Anyway, I just wanted to warn you. Trudy hasn't had a good morning. She flipped her tray, threw her juice box and doesn't want anyone in her room. We cleaned the food off the floor, but we are waiting until she settles down a little more before we change her gown. We'd rather not use any restraints. They cause injuries."

Belle sighed. "She gets extremely agitated when she has a urinary tract infection. Can you test to make sure she doesn't have another one?"

"Yes, we can." Samantha removed her phone and tapped a note into it with a stylus. "We will probably have to sedate her later this morning, and that's when we'll test her."

Belle hated the idea of her grandmother wearing adult diapers and someone changing her like an infant. She understood it was necessary, but it was demeaning just the same. She never wanted to reach the point where she couldn't take care of herself.

"She hasn't eaten today and at her body weight, it's important that she does. She has one of those complete meal drinks in there, but let me give you a few other flavors to try in hopes she'll drink one or two of them."

Belle followed Samantha to the drink station. "What are her favorite flavors?"

"Definitely chocolate. She was born in Switzerland, so she is a certified chocoholic. No chance you have wine flavor in there?"

"Wine?" Samantha's face contorted. "I'm afraid not."

"Okay, that was a joke," Belle said. "When I was

growing up, my grandmother always had an open chocolate bar and a glass of red wine sitting on the top shelf of the refrigerator. Throughout the day, she would break off a piece of chocolate and take a sip of wine. At the end of the day, the chocolate was gone and the glass was empty. She didn't go a day without either one." The memory made Belle smile. "Every time I open a refrigerator, I expect to see that."

Samantha squeezed her hand. "These are the memories you should always hold on to. Share these stories often to keep them fresh in your mind."

The sting of tears threatened to destroy her composure. "I will. I'll take a chocolate and a strawberry."

Belle stood outside the entrance of Trudy's room and listened carefully before she turned the corner. She'd already been beaned by a full bottle of meal replacer during an earlier visit. She scanned the hallway floor and the wall across from her door. No food or dents. It was a good sign. Belle peered around the corner.

"Grammy?" she called. "It's me, Belle." Her grandmother sat upright in her recliner with the table tray locked in place across her lap. It was like a high chair for adults. It allowed her to sit up and watch television, eat or craft on the table, while preventing her from falling or trying to stand up. And it had wheels so the staff could move her around the facility and grounds without worrying about getting her in and out of a wheelchair.

Belle didn't see the bottle of meal replacer Samantha said was in the room. She grabbed a straw from the box in one of the upper cabinets and unwrapped it.

"How would you like a chocolate drink today?" Belle shook the bottle. Her grandmother looked angry.

Belle twisted off the cap and dropped the straw into the drink. "Here you go, Grammy."

Trudy slapped her hand away as Belle offered her the drink. "Who are you?" she demanded.

"I'm Belle. I'm your granddaughter."

"You're not my granddaughter. My Belle is a little bitty thing. You're too old." Trudy grabbed Belle's wrist. "Who are you and why are you in my room?"

Belle decided to try another approach. "Mom, it's me, Cindy. I came back to see you."

"No, you're not. Cindy's gone."

"Where did Cindy go?" Belle asked. It had been twenty-one years and she still wondered how her mother dropped off the face of the earth. Beckett believed she had her name changed. That way no one could follow her.

"Get out of here." Trudy knocked the open bottle of meal replacer on the floor. "Get out. Security. Security!" Trudy wailed.

"It's okay, Trudy. I'm leaving." Belle held up her hands and backed toward the door. "See, I'm leaving."

Samantha Frederick ran down the hallway. "Are you okay?"

"Oh, yeah." Belle nodded. "I'm just emotionally bruised. I guess this is when you recall the good times."

"Exactly."

"She knocked her drink all over the floor. Please warn whoever goes in there next that it will be slippery. I'm going to head out."

Belle didn't wait for Samantha to respond. She found the nearest exit and flew through the door. She didn't want to cry. So she ran, fast and hard. Until her lungs felt like they would explode. She started walking to cool down and then stopped when she realized she was almost in front of the sheriff's office. She could see Harlan's cruiser from where she stood. And he could probably see her from his desk. Right now, she just wanted to go home. If only she had one to go to. Living with Harlan and Ivy felt like home. It was warm and inviting. She belonged there. She believed it in the depths of her heart. Yet she could never return. She was banned from the people she loved the most. They had all rejected her and she'd never felt more alone.

Belle swiped the tears from her face and walked back to her truck. She'd done enough feeling sorry for herself today. She needed to stay busy and keep from thinking about what she'd lost. She wished a vet call would come in. Something, anything to distract her. *Community service.* She had a couple hundred hours she still needed to fulfill from her various sentences. That would keep her busy. Just as long as it kept her busy and away from Harlan.

HARLAN WATCHED BELLE from the second floor of the courthouse. Something was seriously wrong for her to sprint. It was a defense mechanism he had taught her in high school when she felt the world was closing in on her. She paced the street below and for a moment, he thought she would head into the sheriff's office. She disappeared somewhere below him, which he assumed meant she was in the building.

He wanted to go to her and soothe away her pain. He could see her truck in the nursing home parking lot. Trudy must be having a bad morning.

Harlan regretted the words he said to her the night he kicked her out. Another thing he never should have done. He'd taken something broken and pulverized it into the ground. He had let Molly control the situation, just as he always had. In the end, she'd done nothing she said she would do. He should have called her bluff. Molly couldn't handle conversing with her daughter for an hour, let alone be a full-time parent to Ivy. They still hadn't formed a connection and whenever Molly left, Ivy relaxed. His kid was very intuitive and Molly was loud. He wouldn't doubt Ivy had overheard some of her mother's threats. And it was all over things that had happened in the past. Belle had kept her word to him. And he had broken his vow when he told her to leave.

It was done. It was over. Maybe one day he could apologize. Harlan needed to get back to work before he drove himself crazy. He opened the stairwell door and descended the stairs. He had barely heard the faint sound of a door opening either above or below him. It wasn't until the scent of her perfume hit that he knew they were alone together in the stairwell.

"Belle?" He called her name.

No footsteps, no breathing, no sound at all. Yet he knew she was there. He peered over the center rail, hoping to catch a glimpse of her hand or a flutter of clothing. He looked up and down and nothing.

"I still love you."

He hoped that would generate a response. She probably considered it an insult after the way he said it the last time. He heard the door below him open and then close. He supposed it was fitting. He had opened the door to her heart, only to slam it closed again.

HARLAN COULDN'T SLEEP. He had spent the last two hours arguing with Molly over the phone. He felt the inexplicable need to set up some form of a visitation schedule they could agree upon and adhere to. Molly wanted to come and go as she pleased. Harlan refused to uproot his daughter whenever Molly came to town on a whim. She seemed to like the idea of being a parent and talked a great game, but when it came down to actually doing the work, she didn't want any part of it.

She had also clued him in on just how much of an ass he had been when they were married. They'd both known going in that it wasn't for love, but he hadn't realized how cruel and cold he had been by leaving her completely alone every day. He had been pining over Belle and up to his ears in regret. He'd fixated on his own issues and ignored Molly. He never tried to be her friend, let alone her partner in raising a child. Looking back, he couldn't blame her for leaving him. Leaving their daughter was a different story.

Harlan had just drifted off when his phone started ringing. He answered it, half in a daze.

"Harlan Slade, this call is regarding Gertrude Barnes. Are you her grandson-in-law?"

He swung his legs out of bed and grabbed his jeans off the chair.

"Yes, I am."

"Mr. Slade, we are trying to get in touch with your wife."

"She's not here. Can I help you?" He cradled the phone against his shoulder as he zipped his fly.

"Gertrude had an episode and fell. The ambulance

is en route to the hospital. Can you locate your wife and let her know the situation?"

"Yes, either my wife or I will be there. Thank you for calling me."

Harlan hung up, quickly dialed Dylan and asked him to come stay with Ivy. He tried both Belle's and Lydia's numbers but they went straight to voice mail. And he didn't have Calvin's. He called Beckett next, but he hadn't heard from her either.

Harlan prayed Belle wasn't off somewhere getting in trouble. He'd stopped in to see Trudy at lunchtime and they had filled him in on what had happened earlier with Belle. He knew she was hurting and when Belle hurt, she had a strong desire to save the world. Her pain lessened when she took away someone else's pain. And she would go to whatever lengths possible to fulfill that desire.

He met Dylan in the ranch drive. "No time to explain. If you hear from Belle, tell her to get to the hospital right away."

Harlan's gut instinct took him back to the cattle ranch. Especially after the run-in she'd had with one of their employees on his ranch a few weeks ago. There was no sign of her truck. He continued to drive out toward Lydia and Calvin's, scanning every dive bar parking lot along the way. Barhopping wasn't normally her thing, but given her current mood, he'd rather err on the side of caution.

Belle's truck wasn't parked in front of Lydia's house. Various work trucks were lined up along the fence and he couldn't be sure if Lydia was home or not. It was a little past one in the morning. He had no choice but to ring the Presleys' front doorbell.

Calvin answered the door angrier than a grizzly awoken during hibernation.

"This better be good, Harlan."

"Is Belle here?"

"Oh, geez. You two are like lovesick teenagers. You need to stay married and work your problems out." Calvin scratched his rump and leaned outside. "Do you see her truck out there?"

"No."

"Well then, there you have it."

He started to close the door until Harlan jammed his boot in it. "It's about Trudy. I need to find Belle."

"Oh, that's unfortunate. Is she okay?"

"No, no she's not. Is Lydia home?"

"She was." He scratched his chest. "And then she wasn't. Wait. Hold on. When she gets night calls, she leaves the address in the kitchen in case we need her."

Harlan bounced up and down on the Presleys' front stoop. Fear and anxiety coursed through his veins.

"Here it is." Calvin handed him a piece of paper.

"Thank you." Harlan ran back to his cruiser and punched in the address. It was all the way on the other side of the county. He turned on his police lights when he pulled onto the highway.

Twenty minutes later he drove onto the ranch. Belle's and Lydia's trucks were parked side by side in front of a large stable. He tried the main doors, but they were locked. He ran around to the side and found one that was open.

"Sheriff's department," he called out as he walked

through the door. He didn't want to take anyone by surprise.

"May I help you?" A woman approached him.

"Ma'am, I'm looking for Belle Barnes. That's her red truck out there. I believe she's here on a veterinary emergency. It's very urgent that I speak with her."

"Right away. Follow me." The woman jogged down the corridor. "We have a mare foaling twins. The first was fine. The second one is breech."

The woman led him to a large stall. A mare lay on her side, breathing heavily, while Lydia was up to her armpit in the horse's backside.

"I almost have her turned around," Lydia said. "Get a mask and a resuscitation bag ready."

Belle dug through a large duffel, removed two towels and shook them out. Then she unpackaged a mask and resuscitation bag and connected them together. For a brief moment their eyes met before she looked away.

"I have her head!" Lydia cried. "Harlan, get in here. Belle, get behind me."

Belle dropped to the stall floor and wrapped her arms around Lydia's waist.

"Pull!" Lydia ordered. "We have to get her out now."

The foal slid onto the hay-covered floor. Belle scrambled to her knees and cleared the amniotic sac away from the newborn's mouth and nostrils. "Breathe," she whispered under her breath. "Breathe."

"Roll her onto her right side," Lydia instructed. Belle, and Harlan quickly repositioned the foal while Lydia listened for a heartbeat with her stethoscope. "I'm not getting anything."

Belle reached behind her and grabbed the towels,

tossing one to Harlan. She wiped any remaining amnion and hay from the animal's mouth then began vigorously drying the foal. "Do what I'm doing," she said to Harlan. "We need to stimulate breathing."

"We're going to need that resuscitation mask."

Belle reached out and stilled Harlan's hands. She placed the mask over the foal's nose while Lydia extended the animal's neck and applied pressure along the left side. Harlan assumed it was to prevent air from entering the gastrointestinal tract. Belle squeezed the bag with both hands. Each compression expanded the foal's chest. They continued the squeeze and release cycle for a good thirty seconds before Lydia looked up at him.

"Harlan. Grab the oxygen tank. I left it on the outside of the stall." He retrieved it and knelt beside Lydia as Belle continued to squeeze and release the bag.

"Okay, stop squeezing," Lydia said. She withdrew a sealed pack from her medical bag, tore it open with her teeth and removed an oxygen line. Quickly, she connected one end to the tank and the other to the resuscitation bag. She adjusted the regulator on the tank, allowing the oxygen to flow. Within seconds, the foal began to breathe on its own. Lydia attached a nasal tube on to the oxygen line and placed the tube inside the foal's nose.

"Harlan, I'll need you to hold this lightly in place. Remind me around the ten-minute mark. We need to check on the mare and the other foal."

An hour later, they stood and watched two healthy foals as they tried to nurse from a very tired mama.

"That was amazing." Harlan hadn't had the opportunity to see Belle at work before. Sure, he'd been there for a few of her arrests, but this—this was different. He'd thought he understood what she did for a living, but he hadn't imagined this. She was saving lives. He'd never seen her more focused and determined in the twenty-one years he'd known her. He'd completely misjudged her. "And you two do this all the time."

"Tonight was a rarity." Lydia wiped her forehead with the back of her hand. "A very successful rarity."

"Not that we didn't appreciate the help, but why are you here?" Belle asked.

Harlan gripped her by the shoulders and turned her toward him. "The nursing home called. Trudy had a bad episode. She fell and the ambulance was there to take her to the hospital. They asked me to locate you."

"Oh, my God." Belle glanced down her body. "I'm covered in—oh, my God! Lydia, I have to go."

"Wash off first." Lydia motioned down the hallway. "One of you call me with an update later."

Harlan waited outside for Belle. He'd managed to clean up outside with a hose.

"Crap! I have my truck." Belle looked from his cruiser to her truck and back again. "I guess I'll follow you."

"Belle, get in. We'll worry about your truck later." He pulled onto the highway and turned his lights on again. "Why don't you give them a call? Maybe they can tell you something over the phone."

"Okay." Belle stared at her phone. "I don't have the number."

And Harlan didn't think she was capable of looking it up right now either. Between the euphoria from delivering the foals and the anxiety over her grandmother, Belle's hands hadn't stopped trembling since they got in the cruiser. He shifted in his seat and tugged his phone from his pocket. He unlocked it and handed it to her.

"It's in my contacts under *hospital.*"

Belle tapped at the screen then held it to her ear. "Hi, I am looking for a status update on a patient. Gertrude Barnes. Yes. I'm her granddaughter and her next of kin. Correct. Okay. We're on the way there. Thank you." Belle handed the phone back to him. "They don't know anything yet."

"Okay, we'll be there in twenty."

"Harlan, what if this is it?"

He reached for her hand and entwined his fingers in hers. "Then I will remain by your side for however long you need me. I'll never let you go again."

Chapter Sixteen

"I wish they would tell us something soon." Belle sat in the hospital waiting area between Harlan and her father. A month ago she would have bet a million dollars that this scenario was impossible. Yet here she was, blessed enough to have two men who obviously cared enough about her to be willing to sit this close after she'd rolled around in horse manure and amniotic fluid. That was love.

Belle pulled her hair into a makeshift ponytail. "I need a shower. I need a change of clothes."

"You need to move back in with me."

She threw her head back and laughed. "You need to get your head examined."

"You two need to talk." Beckett rose from his seat. "And you both need a shower. You stink."

"You're high if you think I would ever move back in with you." Belle snorted. "I heard what you said in the stairwell at the courthouse. And I believe you love me. And I... I... I love you, too. But you and me, we don't work well together. It's like we live in a baggage claim and it just keeps piling on until we explode."

Belle had dreamed of hearing Harlan say *I love*

you again. And when the words echoed throughout the stairwell, she'd had to cover her mouth to keep from saying the words in return. She wanted to love him freely, with all her heart. But he deserved to live and love without worrying what would happen next.

"I was horrible to you that night. I let Molly get under my skin when I knew her threats would involve too much of a commitment from her. She can't even schedule a day in advance to see Ivy."

"Why would I want to get involved in that again?" Even though it was all she thought about. "It's too much drama. I have enough drama in my life, never mind the fact that you dumped me twice. I appreciate you visiting my grandmother in the nursing home and sitting here with me. I even love the fact that you made a valiant effort to find me tonight. I love that about you. But everything else aside, Molly can play the *Belle's Past* card whenever she wants. And then you're on edge and Ivy's at risk again."

"The next time I'll call her bluff because I want to be there for you every day for the rest of our lives." Harlan lowered down on one knee and took both of her hands in his. "I want to be there the day you realize your dream. I want to be there when you hold our child for the first time. I want to be there when you come home, smelling like—" Harlan raised her hands "—this after saving a life. I want to be there and comfort you after you lose the ones you couldn't save. I want to be the man you want to come home to. The man you want to grow old with."

"Harlan." Belle wanted the same things, along with permanence and stability. She had tasted it, however brief, and it still coursed within her. But she would never put him or anyone she loved at risk ever again. "I'm so sorry. But I can't. I just can't."

Harlan released her hands and sat back on his heels. "I'll wait. For however long it takes. I'll wait."

"Miss Barnes?" A doctor approached them. "I'm Dr. Rhodes. Your grandmother has a severe kidney infection. The nursing home had mentioned she's had urinary tract infections in the past. Both urinary and kidney infection in the elderly and Alzheimer's patients are much more pronounced than what we would experience. It throws their entire system off balance. Then they don't eat, they don't drink, they become dehydrated, and your grandmother is extremely dehydrated. Her potassium is at rock bottom. She will probably be here for a week so we can level her out, and then I think you'll begin to see a significant improvement."

"What about her fall?"

The doctor shook his head, then held a finger under his nose. Belle was mortified. "Nothing's broken. But because her levels are so low across the board, it has affected everything from her reasoning to her balance. UTIs alone can exacerbate dementia symptoms."

"Within a week she went from remembering my wedding to not remembering me at all." Those images still played in her head every time she closed her eyes.

"Some of that I'm sure is Alzheimer's and some of it is the infection." The man's eyes began to water.

"Wow. Thank you so much. So, she's going to be fine?" Belle wanted to shake his hand but thought better of it.

Dr. Rhodes took a step back. "Her prognosis right now looks good."

"Thank you again. And I'm sorry I smell so bad. I just delivered twin foals."

"You look remarkably well after that." He smiled at his own joke and then quickly turned to leave. "Go get some rest," he called over his shoulder.

Belle exhaled and looked up at Harlan. "I don't know what I would have done without you by my side tonight." He had taken care of her and had given her what she needed. She'd always striven to be self-sufficient. To never have to rely on anyone. That was the true measure of success. Well, it had been until recently. He had shown her that help didn't mean she was weak. It meant she was brave enough to accept it. And she was brave enough to let go.

THE SOUND OF someone pounding on Lydia and Calvin's front door woke Belle from a deep sleep. She reached for her phone and checked the time. It was two in the afternoon. Lydia had given her the day off since she had arrived home somewhere around sunrise.

The pounding wouldn't stop. Lydia and Calvin were at work and the boys were at school. "Someone needs to be smacked."

Belle trudged through the house. She hadn't even reached the living room when she saw Molly's face pressed against the glass. "Go away!" Belle shouted.

Molly was the last person she wanted or needed to deal with. "You're making a big mistake. Open the door."

Belle stomped through the living room and swung

the door open. "If you threaten me one more time, just once more, you'll be the one making the big mistake. Now get out of here."

Molly pushed past her. "Don't be so dramatic. I mean you're making a big mistake about Harlan."

She didn't want to talk about Harlan. Telling him no earlier had been one of the hardest things she had ever done. She wanted desperately to believe in him... to believe in them. It was what made signing the divorce petition more difficult. But, doing so freed Harlan and he was better off without her.

"How did you get here anyway?" Belle asked. "Isn't Billings like six hours away?"

"I took a plane after Harlan called and ripped me a new one."

"You probably deserved it."

"I did. I've done some research on you."

"That must have been an interesting read." Belle braced herself for an onslaught of new insults.

"I hadn't realized how many commendations you had received from various animal organizations. Many of which applauded your willingness to go above and beyond to save a life, even when it meant putting yourself in harm's way."

"It's all in a day's work." Belle hated when people gave her awards. The spotlight was superficial and took away from the message to not be cruel in the first place.

"You're a large-animal vet tech. Animal rescue isn't in your job description. You do things I'd pee my pants worrying about. So instead of judging, I should have congratulated you on all you have achieved for your cause. The only cause I've ever had is me, myself and I."

"You can change that, you know." Belle had always given Molly more credit than she gave herself. "You need to swallow the fear."

"I already have, starting with no longer worrying about you being a part of Ivy's life. Harlan says she's miserable without you around. She needs you in her life. And I want you to be a part of it."

Belle had wanted to ask him about her while they waited in the hospital for news about Trudy, but the words stuck in her throat. She had become more attached to Ivy than she had thought possible.

"I want to know my daughter. To do that, I have to make time for Ivy. The only way to accomplish that is to move here. So here I am. I have quit my job and I will take whatever comes available until I can find something at another travel agency. If you know of any apartments, I'd appreciate you letting me know. I'll be at the same hotel I was staying at before."

Belle must have missed a memo somewhere. When had Molly grown up? "I'm glad you're doing this for Ivy. She craves stability just as much as we do."

"Which brings me to you and Harlan. You guys were happy before I camped out in the driveway. And you should be happy. And I shouldn't be jealous of that happiness. I'll find my prince one day. But you have already found yours. And he's waiting for you to come home."

To say Harlan was shocked when Molly called and told him she'd spoken to Belle on his behalf was an understatement. He'd waited four days for Belle to call before he picked up the phone and asked her to come over for dinner. When she agreed, he almost pinched himself.

He and Ivy spent the afternoon preparing a three-bean vegetarian chili and Provençal summer vegetables. They had taken a few wrong turns, but by the time Belle pulled down the ranch drive, they'd gotten it right.

Before Belle reached the porch steps, Ivy ran upstairs. When she didn't immediately return, he realized she was giving him time alone with Belle.

He opened the door before she had a chance to knock. "Hi." She was stunning in a red sundress and strappy sandals. Outside of their wedding, it was rare seeing her in anything other than shorts or jeans. She cleaned up well. She'd twisted her hair up in a casual style that begged for him to release it. But he behaved instead. "You look amazing."

"Thank you. So do you."

Harlan's idea of dress casual was his best pair of Wranglers, a white button-down dress shirt and his black boots. He'd opted to forgo the hat and felt naked and vulnerable without it. But that was all right. A large dose of vulnerability was in order.

He held the screen door open for her as she entered the kitchen. "Something smells wonderful. Did you order out?"

Harlan laughed, not sure quite how to take that. "No, Ivy and I cooked for you. We scoured a couple hundred vegetarian recipes online before we found two we could handle. She helped me shop and prep, and she set the table all by herself. Including the flowers. Those are from her."

"How sweet." Belle glanced around the room. "Where is she?"

"Upstairs." Harlan poured two glasses of Riesling and handed one to her. "She ran up when she saw you pull in. My best guess is she's giving us time to talk. And we do need to talk, Belle."

"Yes, we do," Belle said. "This is a delightful surprise."

"I read that the wine paired well with dinner."

"You really did do your homework."

Harlan nodded. "I felt I owed you that and so much more. I was so busy judging you, playing the good cop, I didn't see what was right in front of me. And I'm sorry about the other night in the hospital. It wasn't fair of me to declare my love for you in the middle of a crisis. Our relationship was the last thing on your mind and rightfully so."

"Well, that and the fact I stunk." Belle wrinkled her nose. "I wasn't exactly feeling my best."

"How about now? How are you feeling?"

"Much more human, thank you. I owe you an apology myself." Belle set her glass on the table. "I've made some really bad choices and some really difficult ones. Sometimes there's a fine line between the two. I'm sorry I put you in the position where your daughter was threatened. I'll spend the rest of my life regretting it."

Harlan set his own glass down and led her to the living room. "Speaking of the rest of your life, there's something I want to show you."

"You have a fire going?" Belle asked. "It's really warm out today."

Harlan removed an envelope from the mantel and handed it to Belle. "This is for you."

She opened the envelope and peeked inside. "The land contract?"

"Pull it out, there's more in there." Harlan moved closer to her.

All humor slid from her face. "Our divorce petition? Really? What are you telling me?"

Harlan took the paperwork from her and held up the land contract. "This is my wedding present to you. I want you to have that land. And before you say no, I heard Lydia made an offer on another property and that's fine. Either way, I want you to own half of this ranch." Harlan waved the divorce petition in his other hand. "There's a major benefit to having a judge as a father-in-law. He was able to intercept these before they were filed." Harlan tossed them into the fire. "Belle Barnes. I refuse to end this marriage. I want you back home, where you belong."

"Slade."

"What?"

"It's Slade. I am your wife, right?"

In two strides, he closed the distance between them. He cupped her chin and placed a soft kiss upon her lips. "I love you, Belle Slade."

"I love you, too. And I already love the wonderful life we are going to share together."

The sound of bare feet smacking the stairs grew louder until it stopped behind Harlan. Tiny hands pushed between them as Ivy wrapped her arms around Belle's waist. "Daddy, Belle's home."

"That she is." Harlan thought his heart would burst

at the sight of his daughter and Belle together again. "I'm sure we'll make a lot of mistakes over the years, but I promise to always love you and work through whatever problems come our way. As long as the three of us have each other, we'll never want for anything."

"The four of us." Belle smiled.

Harlan laughed. "How could I have possibly forgotten about Elvis?"

"Oh, well in that case, you better make that the five of us." Belle reached for his hand and placed it on her lower abdomen.

Harlan sank to his knees and kissed her belly. Belle was carrying his child. *Their child.*

"Daddy, why are you crying?"

Belle held out her hand to Ivy. "Because your daddy just found out you're going to be a big sister."

* * * * *

Don't miss the next book in Amanda Renee's
SADDLE RIDGE, MONTANA *miniseries,*
A SNOWBOUND COWBOY CHRISTMAS,
coming November 2017 from
Harlequin Western Romance!

HARLEQUIN®

Western Romance

Available August 1, 2017

#1653 TEXAS REBELS: PAXTON

Texas Rebels • by Linda Warren

Paxton Rebel was the brother destined to never settle down. When he falls hard for Remi Roberts, he gets more than he bargained for...because she's in the middle of adopting a child.

#1654 COWBOY DOCTOR

Sapphire Mountain Cowboys • by Rebecca Winters

The first call Roce Clayton receives after setting up his veterinarian business on his family's ranch is quite serious. A horse's life is in jeopardy...and so is the life of a beautiful stranger, Tracey Marcroft.

#1655 HER COWBOY BOSS

Hope, Montana • by Patricia Johns

Working at the Harmon Ranch to meet the owner—her biological father—is the craziest idea Avery Southerly has ever had. Even worse: falling for her boss, ranch manager Hank Granger!

#1656 THE RANCHER'S MIRACLE BABY

Men of Raintree Ranch • by April Arrington

When rancher Alex Weston takes in Tammy Jenkins and an orphaned baby during a storm, his quiet life is turned upside down. Falling for his temporary family was never part of the plan!

Get 2 Free Books,
Plus 2 Free Gifts—
just for trying the Reader Service!

HARLEQUIN®
Western Romance

SPECIAL EXCERPT FROM

⊕ HARLEQUIN®
™

Western Romance

*Paxton Rebel was the brother destined to never settle
down. When he falls hard for Remi Roberts, he gets
more than he bargained for...because she's in the
middle of adopting a child.*

*Read on for a sneak preview of
TEXAS REBELS: PAXTON,
the next book in Linda Warren's
TEXAS REBELS miniseries.*

"What are you doing letting a Rebel into your house?" Remi
turned on her grandmother.

Miss Bertie shrugged. "I have nothing against the
Rebels."

"John Rebel killed my father. Have you forgotten that?"

Oh, *crap*. It dawned on Paxton for the first time. This had
to be Ezra McCray's daughter.

"Okay, missy, I'm not standing here and letting you paint
your father as a saint. Everyone in this town was scared of
him. And in case you've forgotten, he tried to kill two of the
Rebel boys."

"I'd rather not talk about this, and I'd rather not talk to
him." She nodded toward Paxton.

"Do you know what he's doing here?" Miss Bertie asked.

"No."

"He helped me haul my calves to the auction barn today."

"Gran—"

Paxton had had enough. He wasn't stepping into this land
mine. He handed Miss Bertie the papers. "You can pick up
your check tomorrow afternoon." He tipped his hat. "It's
been a pleasure."

"Wait a minute. I want to look at this," Miss Bertie called, and he forced himself to stop and turn around. "I have to find my glasses." She disappeared down a hallway.

Remi stepped farther into the room. "What are you doing here?"

"Your grandmother just told you. I hauled her calves to the auction."

"There was no need."

"Oh, and who was going to do it? You?"

"I could have."

"I don't think so. You're not well." The moment the words left his mouth he knew they were not something you said to a woman. And he was right. Her sea-green eyes simmered with anger.

She moved closer to him. "I'm fine. Do you hear me? I'm fine." She wagged one long finger in his face. "I'm fine."

He did the only thing a red-blooded cowboy could do. He bit her finger.

She jumped back. "You bit me!"

"I'm going to keep biting you until you admit the truth."

"You…you…stay away from my grandmother." She turned and pranced into the living room.

"A thank-you would have been nice!" he shouted to her back.

He walked out and shoved the shift of his pickup into gear, backing up and leaving the crazy ladies behind. He was sticking his nose into something that didn't concern him. And he had no desire to get to know Ezra McCray's daughter.

Don't miss TEXAS REBELS: PAXTON
by Linda Warren, available August 2017
wherever Harlequin® Western Romance
books and ebooks are sold.

www.Harlequin.com

Reward the book lover in you!

Earn points from all your Harlequin book purchases from wherever you shop.

Turn your points into *FREE BOOKS* of your choice
OR
EXCLUSIVE GIFTS from your favorite authors or series.

Join for FREE today at
www.HarlequinMyRewards.com.

Harlequin My Rewards is a free program (no fees) without any commitments or obligations.

MYR17

LOVE
Harlequin
romance?

Join our Harlequin community to share your thoughts and connect with other romance readers!

Be the first to find out about promotions, news, and exclusive content!

Sign up for the Harlequin e-newsletter and download a free book from any series at

www.TryHarlequin.com

CONNECT WITH US AT:

Harlequin.com/Community

 Facebook.com/HarlequinBooks

 Twitter.com/HarlequinBooks

 Instagram.com/HarlequinBooks

 Pinterest.com/HarlequinBooks

ReaderService.com

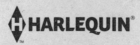

**ROMANCE WHEN
YOU NEED IT**

HSOCIAL2017